'All Season's' Writing Group

Another collection of funny stories, poems, and anecdotes from enthusiastic members of

'All Seasons' Writing Group.

If you liked our first two books, we think you are in for another enjoyable read.

Also, by Cilla Shiels:

- An Everyday Housewife
- Friendship, the Greatest Gift of All
- Jon's Demons with Dyslexia
- All In a Day's Work
- After Mike...
- Management Without Tears...
- 'All Seasons' Writing Group Vol. 1
- 'All Seasons' Writing Group Vol. 2
- Lucky the Ladybird
- Things Men Say
- Zoe the Zebra
- Farmer Bow's Winning Ways

We again, dedicate this book to Dave Thompson, MBE DL MBA.

Dave is the founder and event co-ordinator of Disability Awareness Day, the world's largest voluntary led pan disability annual event. In 1991 he was a co-founder and today he is Chief Executive of Warrington Disability Partnership, a user led charity that delivers 28 mobility and independent living service

Dave is a regular speaker at conferences across the UK and he is a visiting lecturer at various Universities. He has presented Disability Equality training to over 50,000 people.

Thanks Dave,

'All Seasons' Writing Group

Hello, we've been toiling away again, putting pen to paper so we could share many of the articles, poems, and short stories we've written during our time together.

Many of the topics we write about are from our weekly writing exercises. You will notice several versions of the same suggested themes which add interest and show the diversity within the group.

For many of us, we enjoyed seeing our work published for the first time in Volumes One and Two, which has spurred us on to continue our writing.

We hope you enjoy reading this book.

'All Seasons' Writing Group

(All Royalties donated to Warrington Disability Partnership).

'All Seasons' Writing Group Authors:

- Barbara Park
- Joan Isherwood
- Donna Roscoe
- Barrie Fearnley
- Beryl Loy
- Karen Wadsworth
- John Timmis
- Janette Strautina
- Cilla Shiels

Guest Author: Esther Lyons

All members of 'All Seasons' Writing Group have asserted their right to be identified as the author of their work in accordance with the Copyright, Design and Patents Act 1988.

All Rights Reserved

No part of this book shall be printed or circulated without the written consent of the fore-mentioned named authors.

Copyright © 2022

Index

Preface…………………………………..John Timmis	16
'The Lottery Ticket………………..Karen Wadsworth	18
'Fat and Thin…………………………….Cilla Shiels	21
The Ibby Stick…………………………..John Timmis	23
I Wish I Had Known…………………..Janette Stratina	24
You Win……………………….......Joan Isherwood	25
World War 1 Poetry…………………...Donna Roscoe	26
Comeuppance……………………………Cilla Shiels	27
Musical Holiday……………………………Beryl Loy	30
My Thoughts on Saturday.(Joan Isherwood's Mother)	32
The Marbury Lady Statue………….Karen Wadsworth	34
Shorts……………………………Janette Strautina	35
The Marbury Lady Statue…………….Donna Roscoe	36
Just as Beautiful in Death………….Karen Wadsworth	37
Past Life……………………… …Karen Wadsworth	40
What is War Good For?………....……..Beryl Loy	41
Eyes……………………………….Donna Roscoe	43
Why Me?..Joan Isherwood	44
Swan Song………………………Karen Wadsworth	45

Growing Older......................................Joan Isherwood 46

Swan Song...Cilla Shiels 47

Deserving..................................Karen Wadsworth 48

Porky and Spike...................................Beryl Loy 49

A Day to Remember............................Cilla Shiels 50

The Travelling Fair.......................Karen Wadsworth 52

The Fairground.................................Cilla Shiels 54

Toffee-nosed............................Karen Wadsworth 57

The Fairground...............................Barbara Park 58

The Alternative Nursery Rhyme... Karen Wadsworth 59

The Fair Comes to Town...................Barrie Fearnley 60

The Fairground.............................John Timmis 62

The Fairground..............................Donna Roscoe 64

Surprise...................................Karen Wadsworth 65

The Fairground...........................Joan Isherwood 66

The Knife...................................John Timmis 68

Guess Who?..Cilla Shiels 69

Time Runs Away......................Karen Wadsworth 71

Time..Donna Roscoe 73

Time..John Timmis 74

A Handheld Melting Fob Watch……….Joan Isherwood	75
Winter Weather……………………………Beryl Loy	77
Presumed Dead……………………………..Cilla Shiels	78
Conflicting English Language……………...Cilla Shiels	80
Summer Cold………………………..Karen Wadsworth	81
The Noose……………………………...John Timmis	83
The Leaf………………………………......Joan Isherwood	85
Sharing……………………………………..Cilla Shiels	86
A Child's Introduction to Sharing……..Joan Isherwood	89
The Shed……………………………….John Timmis	91
A Moment Frozen in Time…………………..Beryl Loy	94
Duck-8 ………………………………....John Timmis	96
The Wheel……………………………..Joan Isherwood	98
When I Close My Eyes…………………..John Timmis	99
When I Close My Eyes……………….,Donna Roscoe	102
Tommy's Birthday Surprise………..Karen Wadsworth	103
Best Friend's Text…………………………...Cilla Shiels	106
On the Edge……………………….Karen Wadsworth	107
Tales from the Old Four-poster bed……….Cilla Shiels	109
The Edge……………………………….......Cilla Shiels	110

Throwing Good Money After Bad……..Joan Isherwood 113

Stan the Stag…………………………………….Cilla Shiels 114

Talking Stag…………………………….Donna Roscoe 116

Just Like Mum……………………………Cilla Shiels 117

Monarch of the Glen…………………..Barrie Fearnley 118

The Stag……………………………………...John Timmis 120

As Darkness Falls…………………..Karen Wadsworth 121

As Darkness Falls…………………...Janette Strautina 122

As Darkness Fall………………………….Cilla Shiels 123

Who Am I Today?………………………Esther Lyons 125

A Bug……………………………….Karen Wadsworth 127

A Bug……………………………………..Cilla Shiels 129

Three Blind Mice………………………..Donna Roscoe 133

The Bug……………………………………John Timmis 134

My Favourite Book(s)…………………..Barbara Park 137

Escapism……………………………..Joan Isherwood 138

The Tree………………………………………Cilla Shiels 139

The Tree of Life……………………..Joan Isherwood 140

The Phoenix Tree…………………..Karen Wadsworth 141

The Oak Tree………………………..Janette Strautina 143

14

The Oak Tree…………………………….....Beryl Loy	144
A Mother's Wish……………………Karen Wadsworth	147
More Than Just a Hairdresser…………..Joan Isherwood	148
Elastic Bands……………………………...Esther Lyons	150
My First School………………………Janette Strautina	151
My First School……………………………Cilla Shiels	152
My First School………………………….Donna Roscoe	154
My First School…………………………...John Timmis	157
The Shedding Ring…………………..Karen Wadsworth	160
Pebbles……………………………....Karen Wadsworth	162
The Pebbles Picture……………………..Donna Roscoe	164
Pebbles……………………………………..Cilla Shiels	165
Treat a Pebble with Respect…………...Joan Isherwood	166
Distant Shores……………………………….Beryl Loy	167
Love 1, Love 2………………………...Karen Wadsworth	170
Holiday……………………………………..John Timmis	172
Heaven…………………………………..Donna Roscoe	175

Preface

'Sharing' by John Timmis

In the 'All Seasons' Writing Group everyone contributes and goes on to share their own work in many ways.

Obviously, we share each other's company and interest in writing. Much more importantly we share our different visions and as a result, the writing of each of us is enriched in ways we probably never envisaged. We also share our thoughts, ideas, inspirations and how to present or express them to best effect. Should it be in a poem, flowing prose, stark staccato phrases, or some other way? Whatever you decide, honest opinions will be shared with you; your skill will grow. Others will have made a different decision and while you share in evaluating those ideas and presentation, so too will theirs.

Work is read out to the group. A different skill - enhanced by repetition. In doing so its effect on others can be gauged as they share their considered opinions, seeking to enhance both your writing and reading skills by empathic encouragement.

Simple word games are played with their outcomes shared. inevitably, one or two different words will be picked up each time by different people. Words are of course the fundamental building blocks of written communication.

Homework! Yes, we all get it and what we write as a result is shared. We even share in setting it! An inspired idea for sure and there are no detentions for default. (How sad is that?) The truth of course is that when we write our first novel - or whatever - it most likely will be done at home, alone….

Not only are there benefits for the individual, but the group also shares their success with wider audiences and for the benefit of charity through its yearly publication. This is compiled from everybody's submitted work and edited by the group's visionary leader Cilla Shiels. In this we can share a feeling of pride in achievement.

We share the biscuits too - but not necessarily equally!!

'Inspired by Checkov's "The Lottery Ticket"'

by Karen Wadsworth

Jan and John sat in the lounge of their small two bed terrace house. John worked as a forklift truck driver in the local factory. Jan was a supermarket checkout girl. They weren't rich but they didn't go short of anything and were content.

"Hey love, turn the TV over, will you? The lottery's about to be drawn."

"Oh Jan, I'm watching to football."

"It'll only be five minutes, then you can get back to the match."

John switched channel, Jan pulled the ticket from her purse and smoothed it out on the chair arm.

"I can't believe you waste good money on them, the odds are astronomical," John said.

"You have to be in it to win it," Jan said.

They'd missed the draw but caught a fleeting glance of the numbers as were replaced by an advert for coffee.

"Those are my numbers," Jan cried out in excitement.

She could see it now, a world cruise, sipping cocktails in the south of France. She sighed.

John was frantically grabbed his tablet and was searching for the numbers.

"You are sure, Jan?"

"Yes, John"

John imagined buying his local football club, maybe he could take them to the Premier League.

"Chairman of Warrington FC," he whispered under his breath.

Jan looked at him, her lip curled, she'd be lucky if she got a fortnight in Scarborough never mind a cruise. He'd spend it all on his precious football.

John looked at Jan and saw her looking at him with disgust. He could see her now making a fool of herself, drooling over some fit young bloke sunbathing on a foreign beach somewhere.

They glared at each other with contempt. The internet page loaded. John called out the numbers.

"5, 19, 26,37, 48, 55."

Jan checked the ticket 5, 19, 26, 37, 43, 56.

"Four numbers," she said. Her head dropped; disappointment filled her entire body.

John sneered, "a poxy hundred and fifty quid."

His gaze around at the room. Their lounge was small, dingy, and dark, it was messy, stuff everywhere. Why couldn't she keep it clean and tidy?

A tear trickled down Jan's cheek. She shouldn't be working, if he'd have had any ambition, he'd be in management now. She'd be living the life he promised her so many years ago.

They both sat, isolated in their own discontent.

'Fat and Thin' by Cilla Shiels

It was a chance meeting in the underground station they both frequented during their daily commute. They hadn't met for over twenty-two years yet their daily routine to work meant they must have been like ships in the night; missing each other by a hair's breadth.

Fat sized to Thin, just like he did all those years ago when he bullied him into sharing his sweets and crisps. Thin was in awe of his peer because of his sheer size; he still felt intimidated by him.

Fast forward to today and Fat stunk of sherry and garlic having just finished a huge lunch in a local bistro. Thin stood back slightly to avoid the garlicky breath but he couldn't avoid seeing Fat taking a supreme stance against him.

Fat slapped Thin on the back saying how they'd both missed an opportunity to go to the prestigious Westminster school in London and how they had to settle for the local comprehensive. Fat said they'd both done o.k. in government jobs but they'd have fared better if they'd gone to the right school.

Thin hadn't said a word, up to that point - Fat was speaking for both. Just at that moment, a slim, blonde woman sidled up to Thin with a young schoolboy by her side.

"Fat," I'd like you to meet my beautiful wife of fourteen years and our son, Ben who's just turned twelve."

Fat looked at the woman and then his eyes were drawn to the boy's school uniform. Written across the badge on his blazer were the words, Westminster, Dat Deus Incrementum (God Gives the Increase).

Fat smiled, ducked his cap, and went on his way back into the lonely life he'd created for himself. Thin, his beautiful wife and son continued with their journey blissfully happy and unaware of the effect their son's school badge had had on Fat's realisation of shattered dreams.

'Ibby Stick' by John Timmis

As you can see, the stick was emblazoned with my familiar name of the moment; 'Timy' carved (by myself) into the wood. I cut it from a Pine tree branch at Sandiway Scout Camp more than half a century ago (1963 to be precise). Two feet long, something of a silly talisman at the time, it had no particular use or even raison d'être. I guess I just had to be different - no-one else had one!

The mid to late teen years which followed was a phrenetic time of moving around studying, digs, flat sharing etc. Towards the end of that time my father died, and mum continued to live in the family home for many years. During those years I left the Scouts and my Ibby stick 'disappeared' - presumed lost - not that I gave it a second thought anyway!

Over the ensuing years - along with my wife - I stayed with Mum on many occasions and I was aware that, at bedtime she warmed her bed with an electric fan heater! (Yes, the mind boggles!). One night, when she was on the phone, she asked me to turn it off for her. Imagine my surprise to discover that my Ibby stick was propping up the bedclothes so that hot air could get between those covers and the sheet.

In answer to my astonished query, she explained.

"After your dad died, I found the bed cold - particularly in that first Winter. There were no hot water-bottles left in the house after all of you had left so I used the fan-heater. I was lucky that I found this stick in your old bedroom. It was perfect for the job. I've been using it ever since."
So, the product of a stupid teenage whim served my Mum every day (in Winter at least) for the best part of 40 years. Wow! Who would have guessed?

'I Wish I Had Known' by Janette Strautina

I wish I had known.
That where the beginning is easy and smooth
The ending is hard and painful - this is the truth.
And if it starts with a broken heart,
with disability and shame,
then happy end will be the glorifying game.
But not for me-
I will only feel the pain
and walk in shadows of your fame.

'You Win' by Joan Isherwood

Ominous is what springs to mind,
Sinister of a fearful kind.
As he peeks through shuttered blind,
The clock at midnight peeled its chime.

Suited, booted was his style,
No indication he was vile.
His charming front was practised guile,
In utmost stealth – release the vial.

His eyes were firmly fixed on the target,
Armed and dangerous weapon set.
Trigger pulled, conditions met,
You've won a coconut – come get.

'World War 1 Poetry' by Donna Roscoe

I lie here curled up in a ball.

Tired, cold, wet, and shivering,

Knowing when it's my turn to go over that wall

It will be the last time. I will never see my loved ones.

I hope my family know how much they mean to me.

I would not want anyone to experience this life

That has been chosen for me and thousands of others.

We just want a cosy home life and not fighting

the enemy, or as we are led to believe, the enemy.

It's my turn to go over that wall, I'm scared there's lots of bombing, shouting, and screaming, too noisy to think straight.

Goodbye world, my time was short as I am 16.
What was I thinking, to join up for my country?

'Comeuppance' by Cilla Shiels

"Oh no, he's here again," whispered Jason to himself.

His thoughts ran wild as he imagined being pinned against the wall, again. Last term he'd been the subject of Jack's bullying and he'd ended up in trouble. Mr. Jones only saw the tail end of the affray where Jason bared his fists in frustration at Jack's taunting. That cost Jason detention and being grounded by his mum and dad.

"One more complaint from the school, and you're grounded for good, not just a night," yelled Jason's Dad.

"What's Jack going to do this term?" muttered Jason. "I bet he's going to give me a hard time again."

The bell rang, they all lined up dutifully and went to their class, heads down dreading the new academic year.

Jason sat down and, predictably Jack sat behind him. Right on cue, Jack spat at Jason's neck while the teacher was taking the register. Jason knew there was no point telling Mrs. Woods what Jack's just done – she won't believe him. How does Jack get away with it? It's not fair!

The lesson passed quicker than Jason anticipated so he was pleased when the bell went for break – time to get away from Jack and all those other creeps in his class.

Out in the playground, Jason, spent his time wondering how he could get his own back on Jack and give him some of his own medicine. Most of the teachers were aware Jack was a wild child, but they had little hard evidence with which to chastise him – but they were on to his case. They wouldn't give Jason their time as he whinged about the injustice of being the butt of Jack's bullying and bad jokes.

How can I get my own back on that pest? I can't let him think he's got one over on me – it'll only get worse when we go into year eleven when I'm trying to study.

One day, an idea popped into Jason's head. He was so excited, he had to be careful to keep the smile off his face, otherwise Jack might guess he's out for revenge.

The die was set. Jason waited until it was time for Food Technology. This was his first effort at revenge, and he hoped it would be sweet. The class were making fruit scones under instruction by Miss Peters. Jason always enjoyed the class, but today he was elated. Unbeknown to his Mum and Dad, Jason had raided their larder for an extra ingredient to get his revenge on Jack.

Jason knew Jack was forever chatting to his mates instead of getting on with the job in hand. He was always getting told off for wandering around the technology room.

Jason waited for the opportunity and swooped over to Jack's table where his ingredients were assembled ready to make scones. Jason opened the plastic bag from home and poured 60 grams of table salt into the flour in Jason's mixing bowl.

The deed was done. Jack's scones were going to be a disaster when he takes them home for his family to eat.

Jason was on a high!

'Musical Holiday' by Beryl Loy

The Oxford English Dictionary defines holiday as an "extended period of leisure; a day of national or religious celebrations when no work is done". As a child, I loved the beach holidays and the water, building sandcastles and collecting those beautiful shells. The ice lollies and candy floss were a must. It was always sunny and warm.

But then a city break became my favourite destination. Somewhere that has history, museums and interesting Sons and Daughters. The architecture is inspiring. Now that I am older still, and a home-bird, I have discovered that the concert hall offers me an enjoyable "period of leisure".

A concert has the same build-up of anticipation as a holiday. One searches for the right venue, the right musical experience. Then, the anticipation and excitement start as the time draws near to the date. Once we have decided where, we must settle on when to go. We decide how we will travel and what budget we can afford. We book our tickets (not forgetting to take them with us or we'll not be going anywhere) and we choose out seats.

When we arrive at the venue our bags must be checked by security before we can enter the auditorium. We walk up the stairs and find our seats. The conductor explains what is about to happen. Instruments are tuned, they drone tunelessly like an engine. Then off we fly!

We forget everyday life for that period, time seems to stand still. We may go to Paris with Gershwin or down to the sea with Vaughan Williams, fly round the planets or walk down a country lane listening to the lark. I was there as the trees sang to the water on a distant shore. It is pure escapism for me as I lose myself in the music and hear the story within it.

Eventually, we must return to reality, and we find ourselves on a rainy British street, until the next time…

My Thoughts on a Saturday'

by (Mother of Joan Isherwood on the sad loss of her Grandsons)

Being alone with one's own thoughts
I've found it hard to bear.
But I wouldn't have wished it otherwise
There are times when One can't share.

Two precious children in your care,
No-one knows the pain we bear.
We try to smile and say, "All's well,"
But grandchildren are "special" – No farewell.

We shall always say "Why was it so."
God gained so much and left us low.
No sunny smiles with flowers in hand,
Now they play in Happy Land.

We struggle on amid life's toils,
Through seasons much bereft of joys.
Clinging together – sustaining with love
Knowing our boys are around and above.

They are with us, this we know.
Your Dad would always have it so.
Andrew and David were the prize
We had won, from Paradise.

I always thanked God for the life and joys,
Those two special children – two wonderful boys
Brought into our lives at a time – now lost
To leave old for new at a terrible cost.

Everything changes – life must go on.
We shall change too – "Thy Will be Done."
Help our boys' parents to find some peace
Care for each other, their burden to ease.

We are the losers – let it be known,
Those children, so clever and happy at home
May always be round their dear Mum and Dad
To comfort with love when they are so sad.

The World is a far, far poorer place
Losing their children, so young, full of grace.
They play now with Grandads. Whose strength will bestow,
Through Andrew and David, us courage bestow.

And when we next meet – the time to come
We shall relate achievements done
And thank the Lord, the lives He gave,
Were not in vain – our Souls to save.

A simple message which flowed from my pen shortly after a tree planting ceremony at the boys' school

'The Marbury Lady Statue' by Simon O'Rourke (researched by Karen Wadsworth)

The intrigue surrounding the Marbury Lady is more extreme and with many variations to this legend. This is one of them. A gentleman from Marbury fell in love with a beautiful Egyptian woman on his travels. Marriage was promised. The woman arrived at the Hall but not well received by family members.

During the liaison, the woman extracted a promise that when she died, she would be embalmed and kept at Marbury Hall. Her remains were kept in a wooden chest in the well of a staircase.

When the gentleman died, the family decided to bury her in Great Budworth Church. Thus started the hauntings in the Hall and parkland. Certainly, James Hugh Smith Barry (1748-1801) spent more than five years on the Grand Tour of Europe and the Middle East in 1770s.

He was very keen, almost obsessed, to build up an art collection and very interested in antiquaries. It is possible he bought a mummy in the Middle East and kept it in a box under a staircase. However, the rest of his large collection is mainly sculpture, books and paintings. He also did not marry but chose to live with Ann Tanner and their five children. The Smith Barry's certainly worshipped regularly in Great Budworth Church; some twenty-three members of the family are buried in a family vault.

'Shorts' by Janette Strautina

He looked at the table and said:

"What's for dinner, darling?"

She had a secret thought in her head…

But she did not say it out loud…

'Marbury Egyptian Lady Statue' by Donna Roscoe

I went on a field trip to find the Marbury Egyptian Lady. She was hard to find, but after a long search I found her. How could I not find a Lady so tall, sculpted by Simon O'Rouke?

She stands towering into the sky, looking over the woods in Northwich. At the front of the sculpture the Lady is depicted as she was alive, but if you walk round the back and look up, she is pictured as she was in death. The rear part of the sculpture is overlooking the walled garden.

This reminded me of the Secret Garden with a green door where you can step into.

I was too late to look at the Secret Garden but from each April they have sculptures around the gardens.

It's a great place to take a dog for a stroll in the park. Maybe this place will become your Sunday walk in the park.

'Just as Beautiful in Death' by Karen Wadsworth

Toby found the body. He was the estate manager at the home of Lord Heysham. The body was dressed in jeans, trainers, T-shirt, and a black hoodie. The hood was up, it was only when he turned her over Toby saw it was a young woman. He didn't know if he should pull her out of the lake or leave her where she was. He pulled out his mobile and dialled 999.

"Police, please ... Hello, yes, I found a body in Lord Heysham's fishing lake. A young woman .... My name? Sorry, yes. It's Toby Marbury ... Yes, yes, I'll be here. I'll go to the road and guide them in ... Okay, bye.

Toby disconnected and redialled another number.

"Serena, Love. I'm going to be late ... I know, sorry. I found a body in the lake, and I must wait for the police... Love you too, see you soon as I can."

Toby disconnected and looked down at the body again. The skin was a creamy and pale, her blonde hair draped over her face. In life she'd have been very pretty he thought. Her wet skin glistened in the mid-afternoon sun. He'd been told to leave everything in situ, so he waded back to the bank and walked to the road.

The police arrived and he showed them the way to the lake. It was another three hours before he'd been allowed to leave. The investigation didn't take long. The woman was pregnant, her lover dropped her as soon as he found out the news. Unable to cope, she'd taken a cocktail of tablets and vodka, and walked into the lake. A note was found in her bag where she had discarded it farther round the lake edge.

Some months later the face still stayed with Toby, haunted him almost. Breakfast time Toby was again thinking about the young woman.

"Toby?" Serena huffed when he didn't answer, she barked out his name. "Toby."

"Sorry Love, miles away." He refocused on her face. "Yes? I'm listening."

"You're seeing her again, aren't you?"

"Yes."

"I've got an idea. Carve her. It'll help, I'm sure."

Toby's eyes glazed over as he thought about what Serena said, then he smiled.

"You're right. I know exactly which piece of wood to use. Thanks, Love."

Toby kissed his wife and ran out to his workshop. It was late in the evening; he'd been working feverishly all day. It was as if someone else had been using his hands to bring the carving to life. First the chainsaw and then the finer details with the chisels. When Toby had finished it was like he'd woken from a trance. He looked at the carving, her face was beautiful, even in death.

He called for Serena. "Toby she's beautiful."

"Yes, she is. I'm going to put it by the lake, where I found her. I think she'll be free then.

They stood looking at her, arms wrapped round each other.

"More to the point, you'll be free again as well," Serena said, smiling at her husband.

'Past Life' by Karen Wadsworth

Every Sunday morning all the family were sent for a stroll. When my cousin came with us, I would regale here with tales of four hundred years ago when I was a boy in China. Wooden Houses, earth roads and oxen pulling carts, piled high with goods. I could see it, smell it, feel it.

Everyone thought I had made the stories up, but I was never sure.

Maybe it was a past life!

'What is War Good for?' by Beryl Loy

The man asked, 'What is war good for?

I don't want to think about war.

I don't want to talk about war.

It starts at their club, the Walrus men.

They've had their three score years and ten.

They decide on battalions, and when.

Troops and troops of naïve stalwarts.

Regiments, conscripts of Braveheart's.

Walrus bank accounts get kick-start!

Walrus demand gold, they demand oil.

They demand gas, they demand soil.

They demand bone and blood to boil.

I would rather starve than deploy

one bullet that could fell a young boy.

While Walrus dines at the Savoy.

They are white-washed sepulchers.

A wake of greedy vultures!

Against all color, creed, and cultures.

'Ban the Bomb', was our only power.

We did our best, and there was that flower.

But there's no bomb big enough for their Ivory Tower.

'Eyes' by Donna Roscoe

I try to work but my eyes can't see

My hands become my eyes you will see

It creates the work that you can see

To you it may not mean a thing but to me

It's my whole world you see

With crippled hands it is hard to create

With failing eyes, we can only listen

If our ears may need a loudspeaker

To help us with our creation

'Why Me?!' By Joan Isherwood

"One in one thousand," said the Doc.
Fame at last – now just take stock.
The trouble is there <u>is</u> no cure,
The symptoms varied and unsure.

"Why me?" I ask – indeed demand,
It's like I'm guilty – on remand.
This nasty illness knows no bounds,
My head is spinning as it pounds.

I join a group – we all now suffer.
But their support acts as a buffer.
So many kind and caring Souls,
All walks of life, in many roles.

I've learnt so much along the way,
Resilience now comes into play.
For those of you who need to know
Meniere's, with dizzy vertigo.

'Swan Song' by Karen Wadsworth

Malachite sat on the ridge of the Volcano, below a lake of larva bubbled gently. He had lived a thousand years and now it was time for the last dragon of this world to die.

He looked back on his life and smiled. He'd enjoyed toying with the people, but it ensured he would live forever in the myths and legends of mankind.

He was the dragon St George thought he'd slain. As if St Margaret of Antioch could harm him with a mere prayer. He was Zmaj the Slavic benevolent dragon and the Monstrous Apep of Africa. In the years after the second major people's conflict, he managed to be mistaken for flying saucers. Malachite's supreme achievement was to be both the Loch Ness Monster and Brosno the Russian Lake dragon, cousin of Nessie.

His swan song would follow his swan dive, he laughed. Malachite opened his tattered and torn wings and took flight. He needed the hot thermals from the volcano to take off and gain height. He inclined his body down and folded his wings into his side. Once he was below the rim of the volcano, he curled his body into a ball and 'bombed' into the larva lake.

The press headlines the next morning read, Mount Etna Erupts. The ensuing explosion and larva flow obliterate Sicily, the mountain's firework display could be seen from hundreds of miles away.

'Growing Older – A Ditty' by Joan Isherwood

Where, how, when?
Three score years and ten.
When, where how?
Shall I take a bow?
When, how, where?
These creaking bones don't care.
Where, how, when again?
My fate is sealed and so…Amen

'Swan Song' by Cilla Shiels

Jenny, a 93-year-old travelled the world during her military service. She'd never married but she had a son, born in 1943, whom she idolised. Jenny didn't tell many folks about Victor's father, Brian, but she still held a flame for him.

During the blitz, she took rescue in a bombed-out house with another army officer, Brian, who happened to be in that same area. They sheltered below stairs and were without food and water for 36 hours, with no end in sight of the bombing. They each thought they wouldn't get out alive and naturally turned towards each other for comfort.

Help arrived unexpectedly just when they were thinking they'd never get out alive; they were saved.

Fast forward four months, Jenny realised she was pregnant with no sign of her baby's father.

Jenny was dismissed from service and left to lead a lonely life with baby, Victor.

Her Swan Song, 'I'll be Seeing You' by Bing Crosby.

But she never did!!

'Deserving' by Karen Wadsworth

Peter stormed out of the house to the pub. Joanna deserved slapping; she needed to learn. Next time she wouldn't present him with trousers with tramline creases. In the pub he bragged about being the man of the house and the little woman knew what she had to do, or she'd suffer.

At closing time Peter reeled out of the pub worse for wear straight into a fist. Beaten black and blue he staggered home; the words whispered in his ear echoing in his head.

"You deserve this, and you'll get worse if you lay one finger on my sister ever again."

'Porky and Spike' by Beryl Loy

It was early in the morning and the sun did shine.
Porky was munching truffles and whatever could find.
Spike strolled past, just taking his sweet time.
Seeing porky eating, he shouted, "oy, they're mine".

"Don't worry" answered Porky, ever so benign,
There's plenty of food here for both of us to dine".
"Then shove over, will you? I'm feeling quite confined".
Porky was more than willing to quick step aside.

He'd felt those quills before, very sharp, very fine!
Spike clacked his coat. He knew it was divine.
He shook and raindrops showered down like pebbles of the Rhine. *
The friends settled down to a tasty breakfast-time.

*Pebbles of the rhine-rhinestones. Oxford English dictionary).

'A Day to Remember' by Cilla Shiels

It was a lovely summer's day, and it couldn't have been better for a cruise on Bridgewater canal with our close friends and acquaintances. The plan was to glide down the canal, each taking a turn at the steering, enjoying the beautiful scenery on the way. The day was so calm, and everyone was up for a good time. We disembarked alongside an olde world pub in Lymm just in time for lunch.

The food was superb, and the odd glass of wine went down well. Many of the party were drivers so they were aware not to go 'overboard' as we may say.

Two hours later, we headed back home, enjoying the scenery and each taking a turn at the helm. Such a peaceful, sunny afternoon and all was right with our world.

I looked along the barge and noticed one of our friends' relatives was leaning out of the vessel and enjoying the feeling of the cool water on her hands.

I started getting agitated as I noticed her rocking back and forth, as her speech got louder and more animated.

"She's going to go overboard if she reaches out any further," I quipped.

No sooner said, than she was in the water.

All Hell let loose.

My friend's son threw a life belt, whilst the woman's husband dived in to save his beloved. The moment was tense. Where was this all going to end? Tragedy struck after such a calm, happy event with some nice folk.

Almost immediately, the woman stood up, with her handbag still attached to her arm, spitting out detritus from the muddy waters. Her husband reached his wife and helped her to climb on board again, in the most undignified manner.

The couple stank, everyone gave them a wide berth until we were back on land. We had much sympathy for the couple's friends who had driven them to the meeting place and were faced with giving them a lift back home, dressed in bin bags and smelling like the local tip. Apparently, she'd enjoyed a glass or three of wine and paid the price.

'The Travelling Fair' by Karen Wadsworth

The travelling fair arrived four days before, and Dan had spent every night there. The bright flashing lights, music belting out over the speakers and the aromas of burgers, donuts and popcorn all combined to make a heady atmosphere. Dan had met Loretta on his first night and she had drawn him back night after night. Tonight, she whispered in his ear, to come back at midnight for a night like he'd never experienced before. Dan was excited as he approached the fairground, desperate for more than the kisses they'd exchanged.

When the fair is open, it's vibrant, fun, and magical, now everything was in darkness. The brightly coloured murals of laughing children in the light, grinned and sneered in the dark. The shadows of the rides cast by the moonlight bent and shaped into creatures that Dan imagined following him as he crept between them. His breath was shallow and rapid and despite the cool autumn air he felt the sweat run down his back. His face was pale and clammy as he told himself not to be stupid. Dan ducked as something flew passed his head and he laughed at himself as he flinched.

Loretta had said to meet her behind the ghost train, he arrived and leaned on the back wall of the ride trying to look nonchalant. He saw a movement in the trees a few metres away.

"Loretta? Loretta it that you?" Dan said in a stage whisper.

Loretta stepped into the moonlight. Dan smiled. She was nearly as tall as Dan's six foot; her skin was milky white that made her ruby red lips stand out. Her eyes were dark, almost as dark as her jet-black hair. Dan licked his lips, he was mesmerised by her deep, husky voice. She beckoned him and he walked into the trees following her. Loretta pushed his back into a tree, she kissed him then her lips moved down to his neck. Even as she sank her teeth into his neck Dan moaned in ecstasy as she drained him of his life's blood. Loretta left his body where it fell, covering it with twigs and leaves.

Tomorrow the fair would move on.

'The Fairground' by Cilla Shiels

'Roll up, roll up, come, and see the fun of the fair!'

'Lots to do and new experiences just for you.'

The poster was beckoning Jan to brush herself down and start again after the tearful breakup with Sam.

"Oh! Come on Beth, don't be a spoilsport, let's go and have some fun," pleaded Jan to her best friend and confidant.

"Oh! – o.k. but I need to keep my beady eye on you since you broke up with Sam."

"Sam – huh! He's history – men – don't need them," retorted Jan.

"Sorted, will meet you there after tea on Friday, 7pm," replied Beth.

Friday, 13th June, a beautiful, sunny day, and Jan was feeling rather good about going to the fair.

They met as planned and lost no time in jumping onto the waltzer, the big wheel and the ghost train, all providing the high Jan was seeking.

"Come on, Jan?" Beth said, "let's try our luck on the shooting range. I've always fancied it."

"Yeh, anything goes," replied Jan on an adrenalin high – the first for some time.

Searching for the rifle range, they spotted the Candy Floss stall and Jan couldn't resist the sticky, frothy, sugary treat.

"Oh good," said Beth sarcastically, "you can't shoot with that in your hand. That means I'll be left holding the sticky mess I suppose."

"No, I'll wander around till I've finished it and catch up with you in a few minutes," replied Jan.

"O.k. – don't go too far off, or we'll never find each other in this crowd," said Beth.

Beth took up at the rifle range and started shooting to her hearts content while Jan wandered around the fairground.

"My, aren't you a bit old for Candy Floss?" asked a tall, long-legged lad in jeans and t-shirt.

Jan laughed coyly and gave him a wide smile.

"Come on, let's take a look around while you finish your sticky mess," asked the lad.

"Just a few minutes," said Jan, "I've got to get back to my friend."

The two set off, wandering around the fairground and before she knew it, Jan was walking into the nearby woods with a stranger. The lad, called himself Ged, put his arm around Jan. She enjoyed the closeness, something she'd not had for some weeks since she split up.

Suddenly, the lad was coming on strong and Jan was no competition for him as the remains of her Candy Floss fell to the ground. She felt vulnerable and very scared. She screamed but she couldn't compete with the screams and shouts coming from the fairground.

In the blink of an eye, she was no longer a virgin.

She managed to jump up and escape from the lad, running as fast as she could to find Beth. What was she going to tell her bestie about her shocking experience?

An experience she wasn't expecting that Friday 13th, but in time she learnt she would be expecting her baby on 20th March the following year.

'Toffee-nosed' by Karen Wadsworth

Molly stood in her front garden nudging her neighbour.

"See her? To look at 'er carrying 'er handbag dog and nose in th'air, you'd never know she'd been brought up 'ere. Airs and graces like nowt, that one. Thirty years ago, 'er mother used to 'ang a red light in 'er window. Lik'us not 'er sugar daddy is just that."

'The Fairground' by Barbara Park

I remember when I was young, the excitement when the fairground came to our town. Some fairgrounds were permanent whereas others travelled around the country. When they come to town they had to be set up, usually in a special place agreed with the local council.

We watched the trucks drive down the main street and round the market before going to the place they were allotted. I was fascinated by the compactness of the trucks before they unloaded, and everything taken off to set up before the fair started.

There were merry-go-rounds, dodgems, and a collection of games with prizes to win. We had to save up our pocket money to be able to pay for our fun at the fair. There were food treats such as candy floss, chips and more besides.

The fairgrounds usually stayed for one week before packing up and moving to the next town. Some people would go to different places for several weekends until they ran out of money or decided they'd had enough. It was rent time next week!

There were also fortune-tellers who would come to the houses and tell you, your fortune for a fee. I am sure they would look to see if you were married, wearing a wedding ring, and what you were dressed like. They peered in your porch to see if you were well-off and if your garden was immaculate or if you had a car. They had a set of questions to ask you before they told you your fortune. Looking back now, it was all obvious, but we did have fun!!!

'The Alternative Nursery Rhyme'

by Karen Wadsworth

Mary, Mary quite contrary
How does your garden grow?
With sand and cement and paving stones
How dare anything green show!!

'The Fair Comes to Town' by Barrie Fearnley

Cruelly breaking the silence of a calm summer evening, the raucous roar of a gaudy snake some four hundred yards long rises and falls as gradients change. Its obedient trailers follow like children, not knowing their destination, but filled with the thrill of the journey. Wheel follows wheel, five hundred or more, and each clatters the same grid cover in turn. Each wide side of a fairground ride catches the same branch in turn as the caterpillar convoy passes by. Into the night a blaze of headlamps serves to light its way and warn cowering creatures to run or hop - "For I Cannot Stop".

Not just a convoy, but a small town on wheels wakes sleeping villages. Children fling back bedroom curtains and drink in the colour, the noise, and the smell of mobile humanity en route to— where? Where is many miles away and so, cosy in the trailers and caravans, families live what to them is a normal life; eating, chatting, arguing, sleeping. Thumb sucking toddlers cuddle teddies and dream, while younger siblings cling to their mothers who listen to their innocent sleep above the engine's roar. All is peace, but the goldfish in the bowl on the sideboard is feeling less secure.

In a town a hundred miles away, daybreak sees flyers and banners waving in the breeze to welcome the road train which is forming a circle on its allotted field. It is Friday and excited children hurrying to school, regale their friends with lurid tales of little children being kidnapped and carried off by the fairground folk as sworn to by their parents who still carry that ancient folk fear of strangers.

On their way back home all thoughts of fear are banished at the sight of this new city – the fair. All talk is now of the forthcoming delights of the waltzer, roller coaster, bumper cars, ghost train and the side shows: coconut shy, rifle range, hook the duck, ball in bucket and the scary freak show guaranteed to give a few sleepless nights. All this and healthy food as well: hot dogs, burgers, chips and of course candy floss.

On that evening children and parents alike will see, as darkness falls the true magic begin, as powerful generators give life to bank after brilliant bank of coloured bulbs and the whole fairy-tale scene is bathed in glistening light.

The fair has come to town.

'The Fairground' by John Timmis

Elaine glanced at the clock. It was past eleven - time for Toby's outing. She decided that they would go through the field as they often did. 'It'll smell nice after yesterday's rain', she thought to herself.

She lifted Toby carefully from his cot, holding his head gently, grimacing as she lowered him into the buggy. Almost three now, he was becoming heavy. There was no resistance as she tucked in his limbs and gently strapped him into position.

Toby's eyes fell open, staring without focus or recognition. There was no response as she brushed his cheek saying lightly,
 "Come on Toby dear, time for your walk."

Toby remained silent and still as Elaine pushed the buggy along the footpath to the field. At its entrance she stopped. The familiar field was now a fairground. "This is our field," she whispered defiantly, more to herself than Toby.

Heavy vehicles had deeply rutted the muddy turf. Elaine found the going difficult. In the buggy Toby's limp body was tossed around with the uneven ground, his head lolling helplessly from side to side. Struggling past a flooded area forced Elaine close to the Waltzer. Here the mud was deep and cloying. Without warning the ride started up. Blaring music, bright flashing lights; cars - red, blue, yellow, spun dangerously close, their occupants screaming with the delight of fright. Elaine struggled to move the buggy.
Then during her panic, she saw Toby's eyes respond, swiveling to focus on the lights and colours and movement amid the noise. Hardly daring to believe, she leaned in close. A little mouth opened; small blue eyes turned to focus on hers. Even above the cacophony of the ride she heard the gurgle.

Tears fell on a little boy's face, tears of joy.

The Fairground by Donna Roscoe

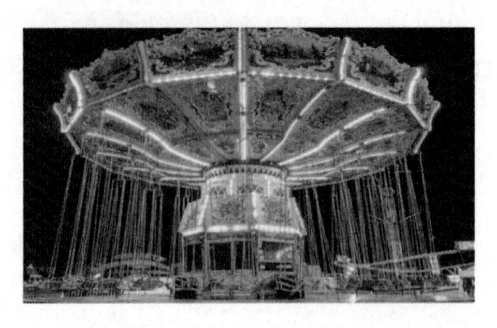

The Fairground can be so magical making you feel so alive. The flashing bright colours matching the music beat while you are going around on a ride. The Waltzers they spin you round and round. Shouting do you want to go faster and faster. All shouting back Yes!! Yes!!

Then you start to feel sick you can't wait for the ride to stop. You get off the ride staggering and swaying just like you've had one too many pints. You say never again until next time when the chance comes along for another fun day out.

The fair is a day out to remember candy floss, donut's they smell so good. Chips, hot dogs, and burger's the lot oh! Not forgetting the onions to go on top.

I will sleep tonight after all the running round the fair wanting to go on this ride and that ride. The excitement and thrills, I feel so alive. The singing and dancing in between rides walking around looking, watching, and smelling all those lovely memories you are creating.

It's going dark the lights bright; flashing music is loud. One more last ride on the swings that will take you up high. Round and round we go high over the park. Getting a bit chilly now tired and skint time to start heading home when our feet touch the floor.

'Surprise' by Karen Wadsworth

Jack peeked around the corner and grinned. "She's coming," he whispered.

Sarah was walking up the road. Jack moved back and waited; he'd worked hard at keeping this a secret. Sarah turned into her street.

"Surprise!" twenty of their friends shouted.

Jack stepped forward with a gift-wrapped box.

"Happy twenty-first birthday, Sis."

'The Fairground' by Joan Isherwood

I saw them rolling into town,
The wagons fronted by the clown.
The annual fair was here to stay
A week of fun, the place to play.

The night drew in, their lights shone bright,
The Waltzer played – oh what a sight.
The organ grinder – and the big wheel.
With huge Marquee, a magic feel.

Just down the road - not far from home,
We did not have too far to roam.
My friends and I we had such fun,
The 'Penny Slots' we sometimes won.

We were young teens and 'full of beans',
Entertainment filled our dreams,
Exciting weekend was in store,
But round the back there was much more!

As this was some time ago,
Animals used to front the show.
Young elephants and horses too,
We sneaked around to get a view.

Small potatoes baked till black,
A bag full off the brazier's rack.
Toffee apples held on sticks
Wrapped around our eager lips.

How we loved that time in May,
To win a prize just 'made our day'.
The coconut shy and rifle range
Used up what we call loose change.

Those good old days are long since gone,
Fairground structure rules are on.
Health and safety now we trust,
No animals to need sawdust.

'The Knife' by John Timmis

"Sir?"

"Yes, Adrienne?"

"Can I ask you a question?"

"Of course, you can…"

"If you found a knife in a girl's locker - what would you do?"

"I would be obliged to report it to the head teacher - have you found one?"

"Even if it was your best friend?"

Mr Moffat nodded, frowning.

"Even then…"

"And he'd be obliged to report it to the police?"

"Yes…" With pursed lips Adrienne turned away.

"Adrienne, don't go -,"

"'S'all right sir, - just hypothetical…" Adrienne replied, glancing back, "I haven't found one - and if I had, I would of course report it without any delay."

'Guess Who', by Cilla Shiels

This hand has held so much. How can anyone know the lengths its owner has gone for success?

The hand has seen the joy of new life. It's seen the despair of loss.

Elation and despair go hand in hand.

It comes with the territory.

The responsibility has been hard to bear at times but these thoughts one keeps to oneself.

One can't let others know the fear, dread and possible outcomes which may not be the expected ones.

Weeks go into months, and the months consume expectations.

The hand knows the expected outcome but the fear of 'what if' remains close to the heart.

The hand engages with others in the pursuit of progress but relies on oneself when things take a turn for the worse.

Time plays a huge factor in the success of the journey.

The timepiece is essential for pacing the progress towards the final countdown.

The hours pass by slow, the anticipation quickens, towards a cresendo of activity.

Just when all seems to no avail… a baby makes its first cry.

Written by a gynaecologist on his retirement.

'Time Runs Away' by Karen Wadsworth

Today was the day, Rosie's exhibition day. Several major art critics had been invited to see her latest creation which had been shortlisted for the Turner Prize. 'Times Runs Away' was a dynamic piece of art inspired by Salvador Dali and Persistence of Memory or as most people thought of it the Melting Clocks picture.

Rosie, a sculptor, had seen this painting whilst visiting the Museum of Modern Art in New York. She'd sat studying Dali's work for three hours, her eyes roaming repeatedly over every inch, gaining inspiration.

Once Rosie returned to the UK she set to work. Sheet steel was heated and hammered into the shape of a hand. Palm upwards and fingers curled waiting for something to be placed inside it. The hand was hollow, two-and-a-half-feet wide, eighteen inches high and sat on a stand lifting it two feet off the ground. Rosie carved and painted a huge pocket watch out of wax that sat snugly inside the sculpted hand.

Every aspect of the display was checked and double checked before a heating element was placed inside the hand. As the metal warmed the wax began to soften and melt. Four hours later, when the exhibition opened, the wax had formed long trails as it dripped between the fingers.

Rosie's work was hailed as a success and would be put forward as a Turner Prize finalist.

'Time' by Donna Roscoe

Feel the time slipping through my fingers

Precious time I need that chance

I wanted to slow down, ok not a chance

I'm working the hamster wheel faster and

faster trying to catch up

to time, where it's going nobody knows.

The hands are growing older and colder

I can't help but stop time slipping away

through them fingers.

'Time' by John Timmis

One day I had a lifetime ahead,
So much to live for before I'd be dead.
Then as the long active years have flown by,
One stares in the face the day you will die.

As I reflect on the passage of time -
Forgotten moments that could have been mine
At first it was but the tiniest drip
Now hours and years fall through failing grip.

With so many cravings yet to fulfil.
Those remaining years seem to pass faster still.
And now with so many aspirations unfinished,
The time left to do them is further diminished.

As body and mind quickly decline
Little now is left of the life that was mine.
Mostly I did as much as I could
And with thanks I reflect on a life that was good.

'A Handheld Melting Fob Watch' by Joan Isherwood

The larger part of the World's population has a determination to survive, to live, no matter how disastrous their circumstances. The demise of Ukraine is covered daily by the media and as it is 'close to home' – being in Europe, we have an affinity which we tend not to have with distant countries.

The picture of the handheld fob watch conjures up a desperate grab for time. A grab so fierce, so intense that it generates a heat of magnitude sufficient to melt the lower half of the fob. These are the fingers of a worker with worn down nails and ingrained dirt. A worker with passion – for whom time is of the essence.

And therein lies the Question. <u>TIME FOR WHAT?</u>

- Time to Live?
- Time to fight and survive?
- Time or organise?
- Time to evaluate?
- Time to prioritise?

The list is endless.

There are many of us for whom time has played a relevant part in our lives. Sayings such as 'time and place wait for no man', are commonly quoted almost as an explanation. When an event occurs. If only we could 'stop time and get off' and, in doing, avoid life's traumas.

Time, for some of us, would seem to be our enemy. Time for others a boon.

'Winter Weather' by Beryl Loy

Winter weather brings ice and snow.
Mother, seeing, smothers us in mufflers.
Mithered with scarves and mittens,
slipping and sliding through sludge,
ankle deep, we are lolloping lopers.
Bound up against withering winds,
we skate, laughing and squawking.
A cacophony of squeals, we bumble on
over the bridge, watching white foam.
Listening to the splish-splashing
as it surges over rocks and stones.
Friends joining the jolly jaunt,
the frenzy rises with the water.
We reach the playground.
Snowballs abound, carrots are found,
Snowmen all around.
Classrooms are warm and entice.
Frosted fingers thaw, we admire the ice
melt and puddle on the floor.
To be honest, I'm glad I'm indoors.
But tomorrow, I hope there's more.

'Presumed Dead' by Cilla Shiels

Jenny received a telegram from the Home Office; "Lost at Sea – Presumed Dead."

She'd wept and mourned for her sad loss.

"Why have I lost my dear Sam to this terrible war?" she'd asked herself each night.

Jenny heard herself asking that same question repeatedly.

"Time will heal!" "Time will heal!"

How often she'd heard that phrase in the early days. But time wasn't healing, she was still bereft. She felt she would never get over losing Sam during the Second World war.

"How could I ever learn to love a man again?" she'd ask herself when she looked in the mirror.

But she did!

Two best friends rallied round and took Jenny to the cinema and the local dance hall, and she started enjoying herself and finding herself laughing for the first time in a long time.

It was on one of these jaunts, the three friends partnered up with three Royal Air Force pilots. Oh, they were so handsome, especially the tall one who kept winking at Jenny.

In a few short, heady weeks, Jenny fell headlong in love with John, and they never left each other's side.

Three months after their first meeting, they were married quietly in the local register office, and John moved in with Jenny.

Nine months after the wedding, the happy parents welcomed Simon Paul.

Twelve months later, Jenny was peeping through the window, waiting for John to come home from his latest flight to France. She was always excited when she saw her loving husband turn the corner, heading for their two-up, two-down terraced home. She couldn't wait for John to pick up Simon and swing him around the living room, showing how happy he was to be back home where he belonged.

Today was different.

Jenny was in shock, seeing Sam striding down the street for what was once their home.

'He must have been missing and mistakenly presumed dead,' she thought.

"What now!" thought Jenny. "What happens now?"

Her mind was in turmoil as the knock came on the door…

'Our Conflicting English Language' by Cilla Shiels

Teaching a pupil about suffixes, I asked for an example of the suffix – 'hood'. The pupil proudly announced: Robinhood. Bless!

Life's tough for children learning about our conflicting English Language. Don't get me started on **to, too, two** or **were, where, we're** and as for **there, their, they're** or **here, hear** it's a tough old world

'Summer Cold' by Karen Wadsworth

Sharon sneezed. "Excuse me," she said as she wiped her nose.

"For goodness sake, Sharon. Use a hanky," Gemma said, and handed Sharon a box full.

"Thanks, Gem. Sorry."

"Are you okay? You look a little flushed."

"I'm fine, just a summer cold. I just feel a bit bunged up."

"Go home and rest," Gemma said.

"Nah, got too much to do. This report needs to be finished before the end of the week. Atchoo."

"Shar-on!"

"That was a bit sudden." Sharon grabbed a few hankies and wiped her hands and nose.

Gemma shook her head and returned to her desk.

Sharon sniffed, sneezed, and coughed her way around the office gathering the information she required for the report. Leaning on a desk here, using someone's pen there, as she collected the data required.

By Friday everyone in the office was coughing and sneezing.

"Sharon, you've given everyone your cold," Gemma said, sniffing.

"Well, never say I don't share anything with you all," Sharon said smiling.

'The Noose' by John Timmis

"Call yourselves the law - this is nothing more than a kangaroo court," the girl yelled, struggling against her bonds.
Ignoring her outburst, the judge frowned and looked down his nose. She was, of course right. The court had been convened in haste. He inclined his head to the noose which hung from a convenient high beam close by.
"You, Sylvia Shaw is accused of causing the death of Archie Fisher. How do you plead?"
"Piss off you pervert!" the girl yelled, "it's you what should 'a been creamed."
"Guilty or not guilty?" The judge's voice was calm. "You must make a plea."
"Plea my arse! I want untied now!"
"Should we gag her too?" One of the men holding the girl suggested. The judge shook his head.
"That would rather defeat the object of her being here," he stated without emotion. "She must condemn herself with her own words."

"Sod you," the girl shot back, "it's you who should be being condemned, faggot!" The judge shook his head, tutting.
"Language of that kind will not help your case."
"My case?" the girl shouted, "tell the court what you were doing when he died, shithead!"
"Your plea Miss Shaw… the court is waiting."
"Won't you even tell them where you were?" There was a moment's silence.
"My whereabouts is hardly relevant to this case." The girl smiled fleetingly.
"No," she replied, "I suppose the poison you used isn't either." The judge exhaled loudly.
"Poison? What poison?"
"The poison in the bottle…"
"Bottle?"
"Yeh - the one you chucked in the litter bin on your way out of the park." The two men holding her exchanged glances then nodded, smiling. The judge smiled with them.
"I don't think there is much point in continuing this charade," he said in a deadpan voice. "Gentlemen, what is your verdict, guilty or not guilty?"
"Guilty."
"Guilty"
"Guilty" They echoed. The judge nodded.
"Executioner, do your duty," he said stiffly.

One of the men holding the girl reached for the waiting noose and pulled it down. The girl screamed profanities and shook herself loose of the one man still holding her. Instead of trying to control her again, the man, joined by two others, grasped the free end of the noose rope. At the same moment the man with the noose passed over the judge's head. In the blink of an eye, it was tightened and without ceremony, the judge was hoisted high where he danced away the last few minutes of his life

---

'The Leaf' by Joan Isherwood

I sway and rustle in the breeze,
An opportunity I seize,
To hide tree dwellers as they nest,
My job now done I take my rest.

'Sharing' by Cilla Shiels

Jean and Margaret retired at the same time, even though Jean was two years younger than her sibling. Jean, a nurse, took advantage of early retirement offered at the hospital where she worked whereas Margaret worked until she could claim her pension from the government.

Both were widowed some ten years previous but whereas Margaret had her three children to help her through the early days of loss, Jean only had Margaret for support because she had no children and few friends.

Jean was at a loss what to do with all her spare time, and asked Margaret if she fancied going to the Bingo once a week. This suited Margaret and would give the sisters time to be together.

"Right, let's agree, whatever we win here, we'll share," said Jean.

"Yup, I'll agree with that, let's make it a date every Wednesday?" replied Margaret.

They had several small wins of £10 for a line and the occasional £50 for a full house. Jean would treat herself with a new blouse or whatever because her nurse pension meant she was very comfortable, whereas Margaret used it to pay something off her energy bills.

It all worked amicable until the day Jean won £10,000 on the National Rollover which was a free draw everyone was entered into.

"'Whoopee" said Margaret, "that'll make a big difference to me.

"Why?" asked Jean, "it's my ticket, not yours, what's your problem?"

"But we said we'd share all our prize money," replied Margaret.

"Yes, for the Bingo games we play, not for the National Rollover," said Jean, "tough if you misunderstood. I'm off on a cruise of a lifetime to the Med.""Right," said Margaret, "if that's the game you're playing, you are no longer a sister of mine."

Jean was shocked by Margaret's attitude, but thought she'll get over it. But she never did.

Jean had her cruise in the Med and returned home to a very lonely life. She couldn't turn the clock back and her sister and niece and nephews ignored her.

Jean learnt the hard way that if she had shared her windfall, she could still have had a decent holiday, and more importantly, not lost the respect of her family.

Sadly, Jean died a few months after her return from her holiday from an aneurism. She'd made her will out many years before, for all her estate to go to Margaret.

Margaret inherited Jean's two-up-two-down terraced house and her life savings totalling £100,000 – twenty times what would have been her half-share if Jean hadn't been so mean.

'A Childs's Introduction to Sharing' by Joan Isherwood

My first attempt at sharing
Demonstrated erring.
Another child less caring
Demonstrated daring.

"Can I have a go?" she said,
Eyeing up my bike.
Jumping on and off she sped,
Just like a motorbike.

My next attempt at sharing
Demonstrated pairing.
My desk mate enjoyed tearing,
He demonstrated, airing

"Let me see your notebook,
I'll keep it safe," he swore.
The pages that he tore and took,
My work was now no score.

My third attempt at sharing
Demonstrated wearing.
The posh girl kept on glaring
Demonstrating staring.

"You're wearing the same shoes as I.
You've got to take them off.
Or you and I can say goodbye
Cos I'm the only toff."

NOTE: WHAT IS THIS SHARING LARK?

'The Shed' by John Timmis

"You're looking great today," Simon said as he passed the neat row of cabbages. "You're not so bad either," he added, lifting his eye to the potatoes.

The shed door swung in the breeze as he opened it.

"Help." Simon stopped on the threshold, listening.

"Please."

"Did you say something?" Simon whispered almost to himself.

"Yes," a flap of felt muttered back as it lifted in the wind where it was torn, "help."

Simon stepped in.

"Aaah!"

"Sorry." Simon moved gardening tools aside to reach the roll of tarpaulin in the corner.

"Ooogh" He heard as he lifted it. Then saw the discolouration in the wood where it had been.

"Oh no!" His eyes filled up, "rot - I didn't realise."

"I did try to tell you before - but you weren't listening Si."

"I am now - I am - I am." Simon sobbed. "Sorry Mabel," he added as he moved the urn from the corner. 'Thank God for that.' he breathed to himself. The wood here was less discoloured.

"Try the other corner Si." Simon looked behind himself. Here another, smaller urn said; 'RIP Linda. Beloved child of Simon & Mabel' He wept as he lifted it, then hugged it close.

"Linda my love. No!" He raised his voice as he saw the hole left by rotting wood where the urn had been. He ran his hand over crumbling wood. Tears fell freely. "I will sort this," he vowed.

"Oh, would you?"

"Yes, I promise - this very day."

"I'd be so grateful."

By evening the old felt was gone - replaced by new; rotten wood cut out, new slotted in; all discoloured wood creosoted to stem any further damage.

Simon smiled as he closed the door after checking for the third time that the primus stove was turned off. He turned the key.

"Thank you, Si, I love you,"

"I love you too," Simon echoed, turning.

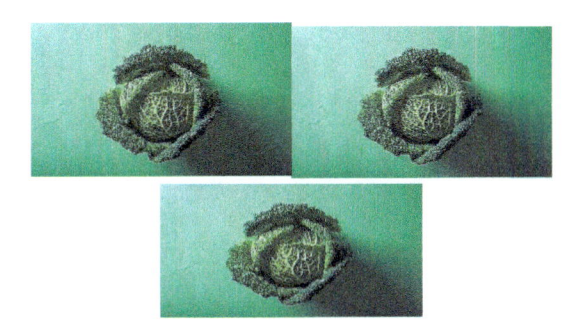

'A Moment Frozen in Time' by Beryl Loy

It was a normal Saturday morning for me as a ten-year old. I ate breakfast with my sisters and then prepared for my usual dance class. To be ready for ten forty-five class, dance shoes had to go in my bag and dance attire worn.

It looked as though the day was going to be fine as the sun shone through the windows. Mum was busy with chores; dad was reading the paper at the breakfast table and my two older sisters were listening to Elvis and titivating their hair. Everyone loved Saturday, everyday life was hard and mundane during the week, and this was a time to enjoy and just relax.

My friend knocked on the front door and we scampered out to her dad's waiting car. A car was something special in our street as there was only one other around. We had an audience of little faces as we climbed into the back seat.

Dance class was in a different hall that day. It was up on the hill, and we had a good view of the surrounding countryside as we walked inside.

When dance class has been dismissed, the girls ran off home or waited for parents to pick them up. I stood outside enjoying a moment of solitary silence. The breeze was balmy, and I was happy and content. I felt as if I was on top of the world as I listened to the bees buzzing from buttercup to buttercup and the hover flies hovering in mid-air. I admired the vista of fields and tiny houses.

In the far distance I watched as a dark grey cloud hovered over a village. I saw the rain falling on that exact spot as the cloud emptied its watery load. Then the sun's rays broke through as if they had been painted on. Above it all, there appeared a rainbow. A perfect moment presented a tableau before me; I stood enjoying this special moment. I appreciated our planet and how it worked. It may have been a run-of-the-mill Saturday to most people but for me it was a treasure, a gem of a moment, frozen in time.

'Duck – 8' by John Timmis

Huge frame; eight massive wheels of steel.
Close to, the heat is real.
The monster waits; poised readiness palpable.
A Quiet hiss and contented simmering mislead
Pressure builds within.

Wires hum through pulleys – the signal drops with
a clang.
Brakes off….
A slight groan: in unison eight wheels move a
fraction as the monster hurls itself against
restraining wagons.
Scores of them loaded with twenty tons of coal
each clang apart with the strain of tension.
A roar of smoke, ash and steam surge from the
funnel like a volcano.
Deafening.
Wheels slip on polished steel rails, sparks fly.

Power reduced – but the megalith moves – just.
Wheels grip; a mighty hiss.
The first single 'whoof' is heard.
The next is louder – the force compelling.
Complaining wagons follow – they have no choice –

Monster has them by the nose…
Its voice:

You'll - **come** - with - me,
You'll - **come** - with - me,
You'll – **come** – with – me.

You'll **come** with me.

'The Wheel' by Joan Isherwood

Starting from the top and reading clockwise:

- A huge invention was the WHEEL
- Today we'd say its no big deal
- But greet with thanks and hearty zeal
- When mending punctures as we kneel
- And so it uses varied and for real
- From practical to such appeal
- That gratitude is what we feel
- Would we do without this
- Waver on uneven keel?
- We're thankful and the bells will peal
- Our loyalty remains the seal

Presentation by Karen Wadsworth

'When I Close My Eyes' by John Timmis

Even from the reception desk Jenny could sense the tension in the surgery.
"Mrs. Allsby!" The vet called from the consultation room.
"Yes Mr Dooley?"
"Can you come in here for a moment?"
"OK." Jenny left her desk and went into the consultation room. As soon as she had entered, she stopped, startled. A white dog lay on the examination table. Its breathing was ragged and every few seconds it made a pitiful noise as its body convulsed. Standing by the dog an elderly lady was crying freely. Jenny was suddenly aware of the vet speaking to her.
"Would you be so kind as to take Ms Alistair to the waiting room, make her comfortable then as soon

as you can phone for the duty veterinary nurse, please and let me know as soon as you have. Thank you Mrs. Allsby."

A few minutes later Jenny was replacing the phone. She glanced at the old lady who was still sobbing. "You, ok?" She asked in a kindly voice. The old lady said nothing but managed a nod. Jenny hastened into the surgery. "The nurse is not available - is isolating with Covid. The stand-in is out on a call." She said to the vet. The man looked horrified.
"If I don't operate, he will die within the hour," he whispered, inclining his head towards the white dog. "And I have no-one to assist." The two looked at each other, then to the dying dog then back. "Do you think you…."
"Me?" Jenny gasped.
"Could you - it's easy - I'll tell you exactly what do - anyone could do it…honestly." the vet said as he moved over to the operating table.
"B - B - But…."
"Just sit there. Hold this tube in your left hand, this one in your right. Then all you need to do is squeeze this one closed when I say "off" then

release it when I say 'on'. D'you think you can manage that?" Jenny sensed his desperation, thought of the old lady, glanced once more at the dog. Found herself shaking as the vet picked up the scalpel.

"Don't do it yet!" she yelled.

"Why not?" The vet's voice was trembling.

"Because I faint at the sight of blood. Do it when I close my eyes."

Jenny closed her eyes tight for what seemed like hours. Eventually she felt the tubes being disconnected.

"Alright, Jenny. It's done."

She opened her eyes. The dog was trying to get up. There wasn't a speck of blood anywhere. Jenny breathed a sigh of relief. The vet shouted.

"Ok Aunti Al, Scottie's fine." Within seconds the old lady opened the door then threw herself at the dog.

"Oh Scottie, Scottie, Scottie," She cooed hugging the whining animal. Jenny saw the tears running down her face - tears of joy - and felt some welling up in her own eyes.

Suddenly they were both hugging and thanking her.

'When I Close My Eyes' by Donna Roscoe

When I close my eyes to the world, I also close my ears too

For I am seeking peace and strength to carry on through

This is my way of chilling out, taking in my surroundings,

Sounds now I've opened my ears again to face and contemplate

My retirement:

What am I doing here, I close my eyes, draw back the curtains

To see for certain what I thought I knew

Far, far away, someone was weeping. Oh! Dear! I find it is me

The rest of the room is sleeping, they found it as interesting as I do

Any dream will do!

'Tommy's Birthday Surprise' by Karen Wadsworth

Tommy was jealous. Dave his best mate was going to Disney World in Florida. Tommy didn't envy where Dave was going just the fact he was going on holiday. Tommy and his family had always gone away somewhere in the summer holidays, but nothing had been mentioned this year.

Tommy's dad, John, had been made redundant at Easter and money had been tight ever since. Tommy was bright and understood the reasons, that was why he'd not told anyone about the school trip three weeks ago. He's also not asked for any birthday presents this year, but his dad had come through on that front.

Months of scavenging pieces from skips and wasteland John had enough parts to build Tommy his first bike. They were going to build it together over the week so it would be ready for his tenth birthday, but it wasn't a holiday.

John regaled Tommy of tales of building his first bike with Tommy's granddad. John's voice soft and the faraway look in his eyes made Tommy feel ungrateful for feeling the bike was not enough.

Saturday morning arrived and his Mum, Janet woke him early.

"Happy birthday, Tommy. Get yourself up, washed and dressed quickly," she said, and kissed his forehead.

Tommy looked at the clock, it was only seven o'clock.

"Come on, get yourself moving." Janet chivvied him along before going downstairs.

Once in the kitchen he tucked into his cornflakes and bacon sandwiches.

"Happy birthday, lad. Big day for you, double figures," John said, smiling "We're all going out to try your new bike."

Mum, dad and Tommy all walked out to the garage. There were three bikes, three rucksacks and bike paniers.

"I know we can't afford much of a holiday this year, but I've borrowed some camping equipment. We need to catch the train because we are going wild camping in Scotland," John said.

"Wild camping?" Tommy had visions of lions and wolves roaming around with them behind canvas.

"Yeah, it means we can camp anywhere. We don't need to go to sites, we can camp on a beach or in a forest, anywhere virtually."

Tommy's face grew into an enormous grin and his hugged his mum and dad.

"This is going to be the best holiday ever," Tommy said.

'Best Friend's Text by Cilla Shiels

Chris spent weekends away with the Territorial Army.

Lately, he'd become distanced and tetchy with his sons.

"I can't understand it" confided Jenny to her friend.

"Don't worry," Shelley sympathised, "at least you know where he is."

"I suppose," sighed Jenny.

The following weekend, Chris returned tired, cranky, and uncommunicative.

He opted for a shower.

Chris's mobile pinged, Jenny checked in case it was important.

"Thanks darling, lovely, sexy weekend. To be repeated. LOL Shelley XX

The game was up. No worming out of this one.

Chris hadn't been on manoeuvres with his regiment. He'd had an illicit weekend with Jenny's mate.

'On The Edge' by Karen Wadsworth

Steve was depressed, not down but clinically depressed. It started when his older brother was killed in Afghanistan by an improvised explosive device, or IED for short. Steve's parents were devastated, then last year they were killed by a drunk driver on their thirty-seventh wedding anniversary. He was alone, he had no significant other.

There was plenty of money in Steve's bank account. He earned extravagant amounts from his musical career, but what was money with no-one to share it with? He indulged in the drug scene as he regularly smoked cannabis and sometimes snorted cocaine. This he knew exacerbated his depression, this, and the excess booze. Steve was surrounded by people that called themselves his friends; friends if he was paying for everything. At this minute his 'friends' were filling his rented home, drinking, smoking, and crashing out in the various bedrooms, but Steve was the more sober that he'd been in weeks. His home was a ten-bedroom country house, rented for the summer before he began another eternally never-ending year of touring. He'd had enough.

Steve was on the roof of his rented accommodation. His feet were balanced on the parapet, toes poking over the edge, his arms stretched out wide. Breezes tugged at his clothing and ruffled his mop of blonde hair. A strong gust almost unbalanced him, and he windmilled his arms to stop himself from falling. He hadn't made up his mind, and he wasn't going to die by accident. It had to be his decision.

What would he do if he lived? He remembered as a boy wanting to be a farmer, the memory made him relax his arms and smile at the thought of happier times. He would need to get clean from both the drugs and the booze. To have a chance he would have to walk away from his career and fame, and it would have to be tonight. The question was, did he have the will and the wit to do it?

He lifted his arms again and turned his face to the stars contemplating his fate. One step forward and he would swan dive into oblivion, one step back would mean a long hard road back to a life worth living.

He stood on the parapet for another ten minutes before a smile grew wide on his face. He knew his decision. He stepped ...

'Tales from the Old Four-Poster Bed' by Cilla Shiels

If only beds could talk, revealing secrets held by their owners! Jane fell in love with their first bed when she married Jack. It's where they had their first cuddle on their stay-at-home honeymoon.

Their first beloved son, Benjamin was born in that same bed. Benjamin's two sisters followed quickly in succession, again, greeted by the midwife in Jane's dearly loved bed.

Jack and Jane enjoyed forty years of happily married life. They'd changed the curtains, the carpet and wallpaper many times, but never their bed.

Apt then, when Jane developed inoperable cancer, she pleaded with her darling Jack that she died where she had felt so loved.

'The Edge' by Cilla Shiels

John always thought he had the upper hand on Gillian because she was easy-going and never seemed rattled.

They'd met at college and after two years of courtship John asked Gillian to be his wife. Gillian was excited to be the first in her group to wed at the tender age of eighteen. Gillian batted away comments such as 'first boyfriend' 'not the only fish in the water' 'too young' 'should be having fun' - she was a determined young lady, and no amount of advice was going to change her mind.

Their wedding was beautiful and came with all the trimmings despite their joint annual earnings not reaching above £25,000. They were lucky enough to find a two-up, two-down house close to their families that they could afford to rent. After a weekend away in Blackpool, classed as their honeymoon, they settled into married life.

Gillian continued working and taking on the tasks of chief cook and bottle-washer. John, on the other hand, played the role of the typical husband of yesteryear, gladly handed over to Gillian by his mother on their wedding day. John started as he meant to go on, meeting up with his football-playing mates for a game during the week and a pint in the Dog and Dart on Friday nights.

Gillian enjoyed her new status and was ecstatic when she missed her first period, three months after tying the knot. When she broke the news to John, she was surprised he didn't seem to be enthused about the idea of being a father, but she thought it would grow on him. Fatherhood never seemed to 'grow' on John, especially since no sooner was Jane born, she was followed by the birth of twin brothers, Isaac, and Joseph. This meant within two years, Gillian and John had become a household of five with only one pay packet each month to spread thinly to keep the family fed and watered.

Gillian couldn't even consider taking up some work because the little ones needed so much attention and her mother wasn't well enough to help. This didn't deter her from putting on a brave face each day and making sure John had a good meal each evening when he came home from work and the children were nourished, loved and quiet.

Gillian felt the importance in making sure her children were ready for bed when John arrived home so they could have some quality time to ensure their marriage survived the unexpected turmoil of an instant family. Gillian refused invites from friends to have a night out as that would put pressure on the family budget. She'd learnt how to cook cheap, nourishing meals and always took the trouble to look neat and tidy when John came home.

Gillian felt she contributed greatly to the well-being of their family, but at times she felt aggrieved that John still felt it was fine to go out twice a week to meet up with his football friends for a game and a pint (or so) afterwards. She tried to smile through this irk she had and look on the bright side of life, but one day all that changed.

Gillian received an irate call from John's friend, Jake, saying John had been found to be having an affair with his girlfriend, Jill. Jake said John hadn't been playing football for some weeks now and it was only the fact that Jake became ill and had to go home early, he found the pair in bed in a post-coital nap.

That was it.

Gillian had come to 'The Edge'.

'Throwing Good Money After Bad'
Or
'Throwing Bad Money After Good'
by Joan Isherwood

HORSES – love them. Own one – never,
Cost big money just to tether.
Age and vets' fees 'break the Bank,'
All to just compare and rank.

Own a share – a mane or tail,
Costs a fortune – it may fail.
To race or jump – the aim to win
Needs pounds and pounds – the bank grows thin.

A pedigree or plain old nag
A stroke of luck when others lag.
The pounds roll in, the bet is sound
With luck – we might turn it around.

'Stan the Stag' by Cilla Shiels

Stan was the pride and joy of Sam's parlour. The day he and Jane wed, they were presented with Stan by rich uncle, Leonard, who had a good sense of humour. Leonard said Stan would keep any kids away and maybe a better form of family planning than anything else.

Jane was a bit put out being given an enormous stag's head, which gave her the creeps every time she looked at it. She was hoping for a beautiful counterpane for their marital bed or some fine porcelain cups and saucers to show off when she had visitors. She tried not to show her disappointment to Sam as Leonard was his favourite uncle.

After their honeymoon they settled down to wedded bliss. In the evenings, when the day was done, they'd listen to classical music on the radio and sit close, showing their love for each other.

The only fly in the ointment was the animal's staring eye sockets which seemed to drill through to Jane's brain. She didn't know what to say to her new beloved husband, but she knew, Stan had to go.

One evening, while they were quietly contemplating an early night, Jane thought she'd heard a roar from Stan. She immediately put all thought of lovemaking to one side and refused to go to bed while the sound continued, and Stan's eye sockets pierced right through to her brain.

Sam tried to dismiss Jane's alarm, saying she must be over-tired, but she wouldn't have it and went to bed in a huff. The event passed and all resumed until the next two occasions when Sam tried to woo Jane in the living room. Jane would stop during their embrace, saying she'd heard a roar coming from Stan. Sam was confused, as he'd heard nothing, but then again, his thoughts were elsewhere.

Leonard's words came back to haunt Sam, and he realised if Stan didn't go, he wasn't going to have his conjugal rights anytime soon. It was with Sam's disappointment; Stan was moved to a more-fitting place as he took pride of place in the local pub... 'The Stag'.

'Talking Stag' by Donna Roscoe

Hey! You there, I'm up here looking down on you. I want to know where my body is. I remember walking along minding my own business, when the next thing, it all went black. I woke with my head up here, looking over all you people eating cream cakes and scones with cups of tea or coffee. You're chatting away, enjoying yourselves while I'm upset and confused as to where I am.

Can any of you find my body? Is it behind this partition wall? They hang tinsel on my horns during Christmas and fire Party Poppers at New Year. What they hang on me behind I'd rather not know. They don't play 'pin-the-tail' on me, thank goodness; that must be painful.

Where there's no sense there's no feeling. I believe it must have been when it went all black I ended up here.

Sometimes I become a hatstand or a coat hanger, and other times they throw hoops and hang them on my antlers and then they all start cheering. I think that's when they've had too much to drink.

Tea can go straight to your head I believe!

'Just Like Mum!' by Cilla Shiels

I always wanted to be just like Mum. She always seemed to do tasks around the home swiftly and efficiently for our crew of eight. Nothing seemed to phase her.

One day, I asked if I could baste the potatoes roasting in the oven as I'd watch her do this manoeuvre many times in my then, ten short years. She gave me the office to go ahead so I knelt and carefully opened the oven door.

I had a lot to learn about spacial awareness as I watched in horror in my eagerness to be 'just like Mum'. The roasting tin ended up on the floor spilling out greasy potatoes and fat all over the floor.

My first attempt at being a future perfect housewife, was in tatters!

'Monarch of the Glen' by Barrie Fearnley

When I was born the world shook. When my legs stopped wobbling and I finally stood the world calmed down. I sat and let my mother lick me and feed me. Standing became easier and now I could walk, and now run and run and kick and jump, and see others like me, all doing the same crazy things. I ran to one to play: he kicked me and tried to bite me. I kicked him harder and made him run away. Then as a tiny Fawn I lay in my mother's soft protective embrace and slept.

Now a young Buck, I stand erect, stretching my neck, showing off my antlers and straining every taut sinew of my body. The pride I have for my very being amazes me. I am invincible. No other is my equal. I am admired by every young female in the herd, and I curse the thought of that old stag who has the run of them. I must fight him: and win.

He charges, throwing twenty-five stone of solid muscle at me. I am winded but uninjured and I fight back. My speed and agility lead him a dance which confuses and angers him, eventually tiring him out. My attacks are quick, vicious, and relentless, back kicking every part of his body until, head down, panting for breath he realizes his time is over and he turns to limp away. The game is over.

For eight more glorious years I lead my herd and watch with pride and not a little humour the antics of my offspring taking their first wobbly steps.
Challengers come and go and are given short, painful lessons without malice. That is the way of it.

Just after dawn I stand on the high fell tops, soaking up the smell of purple heather in the morning air and reflecting on my life. It has been good. But now there is something different, an unease in the air. I sense danger too late.

I do not hear the shot that takes away my life. Neither do I see the death-dealing creature behind it. How dare he mar this glorious beast? How dare he steal my life? How dare he kill me, The Monarch of the Glen?

For my requiem I simply ask: What kind of madness makes it right for anyone to prefer the sight of an antler-bearing skull on a wall to the sheer beauty of a stag in the prime of life moving with majesty through the land?

'The Stag' by John Timmis

"I'm smiling! Ha Ha! But your face says it all. I know what you're thinking. I can of course empathise. Here I am - Lord Dastardly's trophy - mute testimony to his hunting prowess in his younger days. But, like so many before you, he has you fooled. It wasn't like that - not like that at all.

Indeed, I had a good life. The lead stag of the heard I was - had my pick of the does - and many did I pick. Sons and daughters, I had a-plenty. The foraging too was rich for the whole of my 17-year reign. Truth, is I died of natural causes after a full and satisfying life and so the Lord found me - dead. Indeed, I had begun to rot. but his ageing body saw opportunity in my majestic carcass and mighty rack.

So here I am - mute testimony to m'Lord's hunting prowess. Here too am I, on display, mighty and glorious - perhaps forever….

We are both content."

'As darkness falls…' by Karen Wadsworth

As Darkness Falls
An owl calls
Diurnals stalls
As night falls.

Sun sets, its time used
Clouds darken as if bruised
Foxes gambol felling amused
They take food others refused.

Moon is full and shines bright
And the day's switched off the light
Stars peek out at the height
And bats awake to take flight.

As Darkness Falls
Rats creep around the walls
They scurry down vacant halls
As Darkness Falls.

'As darkness falls…' by Janette Strautina

As I fall into Dreamland
I start singing along with birds in the trees,
walking hand in hand through woods
with butterflies and buttercups.

My voice will echo down the meadows forever
with warm smiles, polite chat.
I pick flowers to wear in my summer hat
still hand in hand.

We stride with pace to our special place
to watch the sun go down
as darkness falls.
I let go of his hand
and tumble back to reality
as I leave my Dream land.

'As Darkness Falls…' by Cilla Shiels

…parents are anxious….their 17-year-old's not home

…labour kicks in and mother-to-be is in agony

…the young couple, after much deliberation, copulate

…the drunken driver is escorted to the police station

…the car crashes taking the bend too fast in the rain

…the house, once at peace, now alight

…the baby cries for food and love

…the little girl screams as she wakes out of a nightmare

…the shift worker starts a long, gruelling shift

…that niggle earlier in the day, now a searing pain

…that indigestion, becomes an imminent heart attack

…the lone taxi driver is feared, three louts enter his taxi

The emergency services kick into action each a hive of industry - too many incidents; not enough hands-on deck. Time hangs low, the seconds turn into minutes, the minutes into hours but slowly, ever so slowly…

The young boy turns up safe, he forgot the time

The baby born safely, and all pain forgotten

The young couple seal their love for each other

The drunken offender charged with drink-driving

The driver being treated and recovering A & E

The fire brigade alerted, they save a precious home

The baby is comforted, fed, and back asleep

The little girl is comforted by her Daddy and fast asleep

The shift done, the work heads for home and bed

The appendix removed

The heart attack averted

The three louts only inebriated degree students

Just another day at the office for so many people without whom we'd flounder,

Thank you.

''Whom Am I Today' by Esther Lyons

Before my eyes are open, I can hear myself say

Well – whom am I today?

What hat shall I wear? Whether round or square-shaped

What difference does it make?

I sit up and look at the world outside,

I think, am I glad to be alive?

A few deep breaths and sigh and moan

Oh well, here we go another day to roam

The routine takes over, a daughter today it seems

That is the hat that must be worn, the carer, the doer but let's be warned

The day of rebellion could be nigh, but with my mother, oh dear, no?

Sigh…

Table to set, dishes to side, meals to prepare, oh where is my time?

What shape is my hat? I've forgotten you see,

It seems so long since I tried to be me

I fight for my existence; I convince myself I am me

That fact will not be changed,

I'll say, how come I don't feel free?

My ever loving says I love you for you

How come he can see me when I am lost at sea?

My family, my friends say we love you the way you are,

So maybe all the time I'm looking for this wanton soul of mine

It's here within me staring back,

Through glazed and shuttered eyes of time

'A Bug' by Karen Wadsworth

The house was a beautiful Georgian town house, three floors of highly decorated rooms and spectacular staircase. Rooms were rented out by the hour to the captains of industry, minor royalty, celebrities and anyone who could afford its expensive services. Behind walls and under floorboards lived a city's population of various bugs and spiders that sometimes ventured out into the rooms.

It sat on top of the wardrobe seeing and hearing everything, sharing its space with the dust and other detritus that finds itself way up high. The other resident was a small spider, it kept its distance, nervous of this shiny-backed bug. The spider grew. Bolder, it ran around this other inhabitant, it even tried to probe this immovable bug, but it couldn't penetrate its hard-shelled exterior. Not being edible the spider decided to ignore it.

This strange bug was worth more than its weight in gold, although it never saw a penny of the money it earned. It listened in on secrets, international and business, that only lovers whispered. If nothing lucrative was heard, then it's all-seeing eye captured images in magnificent high-density colour. This bug was an instrument of blackmail, extortion, and espionage.

Its time was up, it had been discovered and like all bugs found in the human world, it had been crushed under heel, forever silenced.

'A Bug' by Cilla Shiels

It was a marriage made in heaven – admired by friends and family as the epitome of a successful match.

Jeff, a pharmaceutical rep, Sue, a part-time secretary where she'd gingerly walked into on leaving school. Sue's long, blonde tresses attracted the boys. She was snapped up by Jeff on her very first hen nights.

"Well," said Jeff, "where have you been hiding?"

"Me, mmm me," replied Sue nervously, "I've just left school. I work at Saunders, the other side of town."

"Well, isn't that a coincidence," offered Jeff, "I work for Beecham's, running round the country, and abroad, drumming up business."

The conversation flowed and Sue had her first dance with Jeff. Jeff was very personable and convincing. They hit if off right away and within months, they wanted to wed.

It was a fairy tale wedding, on Sue's eighteenth birthday. They promised: "Forsaking all others" and made a commitment to each other. Jeff, twenty-six, a textbook version of a 'man of the world' made Sue's parent apprehensive but, they saw how happy their daughter was.

Sue didn't work after marrying because she'd got pregnant on honeymoon. The happy couple were ecstatic at the prospect of becoming parents. They agreed to have two children close together so their offspring would grow up together. It meant; Jeff and Sue would still be young enough to enjoy their lives beyond parenthood.

Time flew by and soon the children entered secondary school and were more independent, exactly what their parents had advocated for.

"I want to be a detective," announced Peter, "I want to find criminals and solve crimes to make the world a better place."

"That's fine," agreed his parents.

Peter's sister had other ideas about her career, she wanted to be a secretary.

"I'd like a detective set for my birthday please?" said Peter.

Their doting parents bought Peter a detective set and Sue, the digital radio she'd hankered after.

Sadly, tragedy struck when Sue's mum became ill and passed away suddenly. This affected Sue badly as she'd always adored her mother.

"Peter, I need to sort out the funeral; I'll be away for a week. I'll take the children so they can be a comfort as well as helping me."

Sue knew Jeff had a business trip which had been arranged for ages and, if successful, he would be up for promotion. They both wrestled with the idea of Jeff not attending the funeral, but eventually, it made sense. Their future could depend on Jeff getting this promotion which he'd worked so hard for; Sue's mum would have understood.

"No problem, darling, I'm so sorry. I'll keep everything in order till you get back," replied Jeff.

Sue and the children were away for a week. Sue and her brother, Simon sorted out the funeral arrangements and put their mother's house up for sale. They returned home eager to see Jeff as they'd all missed him and wanted to be comforted after their ordeal.

Jeff seemed a tad touchy, but Sue put it down to his not getting that promotion he'd hankered after. Sue chose to give him space. but she was on an emotional roller-coaster every time she thought of her dear mum.

"Dad, dad," shouted Peter, "I think there's been an intruder in our house."

'What on earth are you talking about?" replied Jeff.

"Listen, listen Mum!"

"Darling, when are you going to leave Sue. I want you more than anything, I can't live without you. You've got to choose me or her!"

"Let me think. I'll sort it, give Sue time to get over her mother. We'll be together for ever," replied Jeff to this unfamiliar voice.

Jeff stood still, Sue froze, as she realised the love of her life had been playing around at the very time when she needed his unstinting love and devotion.

Somehow, Peter decided he didn't want to be a detective after witnessing the demise of his parents and the heartache brought about by the bug he'd unwittingly set up in the spare bedroom.

'Three Blind Mice' by Donna Roscoe

Three blind mice

Three blind mice

See how they run

See how they run

All over the place because they can't see

The farmer's wife had a hard time trying to cut

Off their tails with a carving knife

Have you ever seen such a sight in your life?

As three blind mice!

'The Bug by John Timmis

"Some would call me a pond bug. Sadly though, most will be unaware that I exist at all. But I do exist, and I'll have you know that I occupy a valuable niche in the complex web of life on Planet Earth. I am a Dytiscus Beetle Larva more accurately known as Dytiscus marginalis. Like my imago, I am a voracious carnivore and though I live in stagnant water, I breathe air. To do so, the bristles on my rear end break through the surface film allowing my breathing organs access to the air above. In this position I can hang motionless for hours with my jaws open ready.

I feel I should tell you a little more about those jaws just in case you are visualising vicious carnivore-like teeth. Ha, there are no teeth in my jaws. Instead, they are like a pair of sharp pincers. But these pincers are hollow - like hypodermic needles. In an instant they can grasp and pierce the skin of any unwary animal which comes within reach. Believe me, it's exhausting keeping hold of an animal which is writhing in pain, trying to escape, so firstly I inject a nerve poison. It takes a little while to act but my victim's struggles help to circulate it to its nerve centres and within a minute or so those struggles cease. Once effectively paralysed, I can take my time.

Next, I inject a cocktail of digestive enzymes which begin the process of turning my victim's insides into a nutrient-rich juice. This all takes place within the animal's cuticle which the enzyme mixture leaves intact and can take several hours to complete. Once my hapless victim's insides have been thusly dissolved, I suck the juices out and discard the empty skin.

The first time I did this I wondered how it would feel to be dissolved slowly from the inside - then realised that the nerve poison might help to mitigate any such sensations. The second time I wondered why I should care anyway. Mostly I just eat anything that moves close enough without a second thought. And that's all I do; eat, twenty-four-seven. That's my life - for now.

The last thing I want to say is that I share this stagnant water with a host of other creatures many of which breathe air in the same way I do; among them are gnat, midge, and mosquito larvae. Given their proximity and my inherent laziness, these are what I eat most of but mosquito larvae - being that bit bigger - and juicier - are my favourites!"

'My Favourite Book(s)' by Barbara Park

When I was a child, I was always reading books. These were given to me as a birthday or Christmas presents by my relatives as they knew I was an avid reader. I particularly liked books by Enid Blyton.

My favourite books by Enid Blyton were the 'Famous Five' series which involved groups of children who would have adventures together in boats on lakes. They would be competing with other groups of children. They would set up a place to have a picnic and often take other people's food when the first group were on the lake, enjoying a ride in a boat.

They would also kidnap an uncle and hold him to ransom. He would go along with them, and everybody would enjoy a good laugh. Food from the barbecue was supervised by this uncle.

I had a very strict upbringing so these adventures in the books I read were exciting and fun. They kept my imagination working and alive.

'Escapism' by Joan Isherwood

Just 'like greased lightning'
They shot passed,
Their paws were skidding
Which one was last?

A visitor to open doors,
They could get out
Hope no one knows.
Then comes the shout.

"Shut that door," was Larry's call.
Stopped in their track
By one and all.
Not today but we'll be back.

We love our home
But need a change,
We want to roam,
And out of range.

Us Siamese are special breed.
We do not wander
We move at speed.
Must stay at home and dream of yonder.

'The Tree' by Cilla Shiels

I'm a green tree.

I'm six foot tall but I'm often overlooked.

I don't know why people say I'm lovely to look at but, when it suits them, they ignore me.

I can't help it if some of my greenery falls off and looks a mess – it's their fault - not mine.

I'm admired by many for a short time when I seem to be in the limelight, but I know I'm not everyone's favourite tree. Maybe that's why they treat me with contempt – one minute I'm the bees' knees and before you can say Jack Robinson, I'm a nuisance.

It's their fault that I can be frustrating, but if they treated me well in the first place, I'd do them proud but sadly…

…they never learn!

Happy Christmas!

'The Tree…of Life' by Joan Isherwood

I've learnt a lot about a tree

Since certain species bothered me.

My nose flows like the River Dee –

Just mornings – long enough you see

To cause discomfort, though I'm free

By noon – and thankful when I flee,

Into town for cups of tea,

To meet with friends and pay the fee.

Back home and there the friendly bee,

Buzzes round a chosen tree,

Seeking pollen – there's the key

TO LIFE – forget my allergy.

'The Phoenix Tree' by Karen Wadsworth

The seed of the most sacred tree was planted four thousand years ago by an apprentice shaman. This place was powerful. Three earth ley lines used for pilgrimage surrounded this land in a perfect equilateral triangle. For those with the Sight the light shimmered over that land. Deer and rabbits never touched its saplings tender shoots. The young shaman, chosen to sow the seed at the triangles very centre, watched over the tree for the next sixty years. He saw it grow from tiny shoots to pliable sapling then into a strong sturdy young tree. This year was going to be its second rebirth.

The first rebirth was two thousand years ago. That rebirth was witnessed by another man of faith, a different faith, a new, young faith. He placed a rustic wooden cup deep inside the trunk, a cup that became a relic of myth and legend. The tree took the cup deep into the earth, cradling it in its roots.

The tree had witnessed people of many different faiths over the years, these people all held the same optimism and hope of a better future for themselves and the world. Women desperate for a child would bring their husbands to make love beneath the sheltering branches convinced they would conceive. Animals that were weak and sick came to graze on the wild herbs and plants growing around the tree.

Its heartwood had rotted out over the last fifty years, only the bark was holding it together, this would be its last winter. The old bark trunk wrapped protectively around the new shoots, born not out of the ashes but out of its composted heart. Born again to live another two thousand years.

A thick, almost impenetrable forest had grown up and around this triangular clearing, so the sacred tree did not see many visitors now. Would anything momentous happen at this rebirth?

'The Oak Tree' by Janette Strautina

Inspired by an ancient Latvian folk song.
Oh, green oak-tree in a Dale,
why did you grow so low in a Vale?
Young children will break your branches.
Playing on the mountain ranges

But remember you, young girls.
Leave the top of the tree to the birds.
They will fly down and build a nest.
Wind will sway the branches and rest.

'The Oak Tree' by Beryl Loy

I was planted along with my brothers, a long time ago as saplings on master's new estate. It was a marvel and people came for miles around to admire it. I used to be afraid of the Old North Wind. Thinking he might snap me in two. How I tried to stand upright, as the wind blew stronger. I soon found out that we would not break, as we gave in to the pressure. Indeed, it made us all stronger.

We were taller now and made a majestic sight. As we grew bigger and stouter, so our crowns became thick and lush. No insects or birds could harm us as we had a secret weapon, Tannic Acid. Indeed, we provided shelter for myriads of insects and birds with their tickly nests and webs. Armies of Ants, hives of bees, spiders of all sizes and colours, squirrels, and badgers in our roots. It was all one kingdom, and we were kings, planted for kings.

But humans came along with their sharp spiky saws to chop and chew at my brothers. There was only a few of us left, sweeping up the hill along a newly laid drive to the mansion. The men took away all the wood to build great oak ships to sail the seas and engage in war, such fools! They made oaken barrels for their wine, which made them even more foolish. Barrels for fish, biscuits, water, and foodstuffs. After a few quiet years, men came to flatten the mansion and made farms for agriculture. Of course, they needed houses, made from wood as was everything in them, for their farmers and farmhands. Then many left the farms to work in the great belching factories of the cities. The country was criss-crossed with dirt roads to make travelling easier. Brick houses in great numbers were built and surrounded me and more trees were sawn down for them. I was left alone at the crossroads. I was an important landmark and so I was spared.

Still, I grew, still I sheltered many insects and animals. When the motor car came along, how noisy, and smelly it was. I didn't think it would last five minutes but soon, there were hundreds of them, even noisier and smellier than before. For seven hundred years I have stood in my place and hope that I will be left another seven hundred years, so that I can carry on sheltering all the life I have under my thick canopy and to leave behind fine progeny for another age to come.

Tree facts...

The oldest tree is eighty-thousand-year-old and lives in Utah, USA. It is named Panda.

Truffles live under oak trees, but truffle hunters do not plant truffles, they plant oak trees and truffles will grow there.

Ten million acorns are produced around the world each year. Some are eaten by animals, some rot down and one per tree, per year grow into oak trees.

Druids worshipped the oak tree, believing that the acorns, which they carried round brought good health and good luck.

'A Mother's Wish' by Karen Wadsworth

Gillian was clearing the house of her late mother. At the back of the wardrobe among the shoes and dust was a box. Inside the box was a diamond necklace and a journal. Gillian sat on the bed and read the journal; it chronicled a trip across Europe her mother made when she was in her early twenties. A letter at the back of the journal was addressed to Gillian:

> To my darling daughter
>
> You may not believe this, but I was young and carefree once. I had wonderful adventures before I let life get in the way. Sell the necklace and have your own adventures. Live life to the full while you are young enough to enjoy it.
>
> Love Mum

Gillian did just that, using the journal she recreated her mother's trip. Living like she'd never done before.

"Thanks Mum."

'More than just a Hairdresser'
by Joan Isherwood

We met in 1964,
Your shop, a thriving hair care store.
Then we lost touch – I moved away,
Too far – my hair went all astray.

You ministered in Church one night,
My hair was in a sorry plight.
"That lot needs taming," you declared.
"Visit me and get repaired."

Your expertise came with renown,
Ian, you are the best in Newton town.
I now can hold my head up high,
My tresses you will beautify.

You've kept your looks, your business grew,
International fame recognized you.
Your cuts and styles made to inspire,
Your young cadets – to now acquire.

Spare time with horses, 'doggies' too,
You do Eventing with your crew.
Your love for animals is clear,
They are your life – all you hold dear.

Your gowns are glamorous and rich,
You 'strut your stuff' – 'a classy bitch.'
Your elegance for all to see,
Parades you love, one, two, or three.

But seriously, we can connect,
And come together to perfect
The funeral of our much-loved Lilian -
A Minister – one in a million.

A visit to your shop is fun,
Gay banter could cause some to run.
To me you are a special friend,
With whom time spent will never end.

'Elastic Bands' by Esther Lyons

Life is like an elastic band

Stretched and twisted, holding us together

Throughout thick and thin and stormy weather

We're always close at hand.

Mothers and daughters are like this too

We argue, we fight, we slam the door

Because we feel we aren't sure

How far our band will s t r e t c h…

But ours is looked after you can tell

It's supple and pliable and stretches forever

Because our bond together swells

It shows our love's done well

'My First School' by Janette Strautina

My first school was a red brick building in the centre of Riga (Latvia) We had lots of homework and had to wear ugly uniforms. During the break we jumped the skipping-rope in the courtyard. There were some characters in the school - a boy whose surname meant "Blue-head". There were rumours that he enjoyed eating chalk and drinking ink.

The school's orchestra held rehearsals in a shed. The music teacher tuned instruments by beating upon the so-called musical stool which had a particular sound. I still remember winter fancy dress parties in the big hall. The school's piano player performed the most beautiful and fashionable music of that time, e.g., the Beatles music. At one of the parties there was a girl called Candy, who wore a fringed dress. Every fringe was a sweet wrapper attached to her dress. There was a leopard with a beautiful tail and a fox.

My mom had sewn me a white snow-flake dress and I danced with a boy who was wearing a Chimney Sweep costume. He had sooty hands, so he was afraid to touch me as I was pure white, and it was so lovely.

'My First School' by Cilla Shiels

My first school was an ex-jail in our small village, opposite the police station. As crime soared, I suspect the powers that be decided to build a bigger 'home' for the criminals in the borough.

There were only three classrooms and a small concrete playground. Each classroom had an open fire where our daily third of a pint of milk was defrosted in wintertime. I never liked milk, so I used to swop my friend's empty bottle for my full one. Miss spotted me mid-swop one day and punished me by hitting me hard on the hand with a ruler.

I remember my first day, I asked Mum. "Why are all the boys crying?"

I couldn't understand why they didn't like starting school. I loved it! I learnt so many skills which have followed me throughout my life,

Each May we'd have the maypole out and told to go round and round it in a certain way, which we always seem to get wrong, much to the annoyance of teacher.

The toilets were two brick-built huts with a long piece of wood with a hole in, below which stood the toilet basin. We had to use shiny toilet paper which wasn't fit for purpose.

Mum took me the first day to show me how to get to school and after that I was left to my own devices to walk half a mile back and forth every day.

Next door to the school was a bread shop with the delicious smells of iced buns hanging in the air on cold, frosty days. Sometimes my Mum would come to meet me to do some shopping in the village. I'd often manage to wangle a delicious, iced bun from Mum's meagre housekeeping.

Oh! The joys of early school life followed me into adulthood as I re-entered higher education to pursue my career in education.

'My First Primary School' by Donna Roscoe

My First Primary school was Sycamore Lane Country Primary school. Mr Woods was Head until retirement, then Mr Saddler became Head and Mrs Harper was the secretary. It educated children for over thirty years until it was turned into apartment blocks. I don't see the need for apartment blocks towering over the houses around the school. The houses have no privacy in their gardens now. Prisoners in their own home (Big Brother is watching you!). I don't see the logic in building more houses and apartments but reducing schools, hospitals, doctors' surgeries. I do know building houses means more money for the council.

So many houses are being built with not enough schools to educate the children. It was a good school with large playing fields. I remember a ladder on the wall with spellings in the infant class and the teacher telling my parents I was struggling with those spellings.

I remember the girl who lived near the school, sat next to me in class and was always pinching me. That won't have helped me to like school. That young girl now is a teacher living in Guernsey, married three children and grandchildren.

My nana and mum worked at the school as cleaners, so I was always hanging around school in the classes playing with the toys.

When I moved up to the juniors, I was taken to the staff room for lessons, I think this was to help children who were struggling. Mr Carter took the lesson, and he would talk to us and help us. We would make papier-mâché, blow up balloons, then cover them with wet soggy newspapers until it dried. We then popped the balloons. I think my problem was depression from an early age. It's something I couldn't get rid of and would not want others to experience.

When doing multiplication, I couldn't get my $8 \times 8 = 64$. I will never forget this because Miss Jones slapped me for not getting it right. Yes, I did cry because it was a shock, but I never forgot it. After that incident a girl who was struggling like me left the school and went to another school hopefully, she got the help she needed.

We had a teacher called Mrs Tucker who was always happy. I remember lining up with my sewing by teacher's desk. I carried on sewing while waiting to be seen by the teacher. I think I got carried away and forgot about the lad in front of me and yes, the needle went into his bum. He jumped a mile, but we became good friends after that. He'd turn up at my house with a cow's skull that he'd brought into school to do a talk on.

Who said romance had died?

───────────────────────────

'My First School' by John Timmis

"Straighten those lines! You boy, - yes you in the blue jumper - face the front, chin up! That goes for all of you. Straight I said."
None of us liked Tonner. We called him 'Sodface". Many of us used a different name behind our hands.
"Hand away from your face Johnson. Now!"
He drew himself to full height towering above us, stiff as a stick.
"Atten - tion!"
I think he liked to see us saluting him. Probably made him feel important.
"Hold it, hold it". You there - Harvey, stand out!"
A boy at the back of the newie's line stepped out of his line to one side.
"A-a-a-a-t ease!"
Sodface marched quickly towards the boy casting his searching eyes over the rest of us as he went.

We knew what came next. Without warning a large, calloused hand crashed into the side of Harvey's head. He screamed and burst into tears. "Hands behind your back boy and cut the wailing you baby or I'll really give you something to yell about. Grow up! Now get in line!" Sodface raised his hand. Harvey squealed and jumped back into line. Sodface glared at him.

It was the same every day. Sometimes we would be late for dinner - all the best choices long since gone - scoffed by the juniors. Their marshall was nice - strutted about with a cane - which it is said, hurt like hell but no-one I know ever even saw her use it - never mind felt it.
"Wake up Johnson you dreamer. Get into step or there'll be no dinner for you."
Hastily I stepped forward, matching my step with Gronny in front of me. As I did so I noticed Gronny's hand went up to his face. I heard what he said, stifled a laugh but couldn't help grinning.
"Wipe that smirk off your face boy!"

He moved closer to our line, eyes upon me. I knew what was coming. I knew too that it would hurt lots. But Sodface'd got no response from me. It did hurt - same ear as earlier – it hurt a lot. I know I went red - but I made no sound. The look on his face almost made me grin again.

I am six years old and already I have learned how a gentleman should behave

'The Shedding Ring' by Karen Wadsworth

Let me introduce myself. My name is Lad, or that is what my partner calls me. My partner is the Farmer, he can't do his job without me and I need him to guide and direct me so I can do my job. I have lived through five winters. I can count to five because when we trial there is usually five sheep.

The Farmer gives me a soft place to lay my head, he feeds me and gives me private healthcare. To be honest I'd do the job for free, I love it so much. I run about on the farm all day, but the special times are when we do the trials. I'm good at them, I've won lots of rosettes. In fact, I'm in the middle of a trial right now.

The secret of a good trial is how you perform the lift of the sheep. I need to be firm enough, so the sheep don't mess me about, but also gentle enough for them to trust I won't hurt them if they co-operate. These sheep have been very good and done everything I've asked of them.

I'm close to the end now, I've brought the sheep into a big ring outlined with straw. Two of the sheep have collars on, bigger than mine so everyone can see them. The Farmer and I must separate one of the collared sheep from the others. Sheep don't like being separated from the rest of the flock, but between us we can do it.

The Farmer stands at one side of the ring, arms out wide waving his crop to keep the sheep circulating. I'm at the other side of the ring, laid down waiting like a coiled spring ready to move at a command. As the sheep mill around, I hold my breath, one of the collared sheep is at the back. A small gap opens and almost before the Farmer asks me to move, I'm in there. Four sheep go right, but my presence sends the collared sheep the other way. I smile as the Farmer shouts at me.

"Excellent, Lad. Well done."

Only the pen to do. I bring the separated sheep back to the others and it is so grateful it leads the others into the pen. The Farmer swings the gate shut and fastens it. I am so happy and excited I jump up and he deftly catches me, grinning widely as I lick his face. If I'm not mistaken that is another first place for us.

'Pebbles' by Karen Wadsworth

"You have five minutes to collect your ammunition. 3 ... 2 ... 1 ... Go."

Five contestants crouched down and scrabbled around on the beach. The man with the microphone continued with his commentary.

"These are the first and youngest competitors in our competition today, the six-to-ten-year age range. They're gathering the pebbles quickly. Whoa, what's Louis doing? Remember Louis is our youngest contestant, today is his 6th birthday."

Louis was looking for a particular pebble, flat with smooth, rounded edges, nothing else would do.

"10 ... 9 ... 8 ... 7 ... 6 ... 5 ...4."

Louis smiled and picked up his single stone.

"3 ... 2 ... 1 ... Stop picking."

The youngsters all lined up facing the calm, glassy sea, reflecting the bright, clear, blue sky.

"One at time throw your ammunition. The stone that goes the farthest will win."

Frank went first, pitching his pebbles as far as he could. Janet followed, then Jimmy and Dennis.

"Last but not least it's little Louis and he has just one stone. Off you go Louis."

Louis stood side on to the sea and bent his knees. He threw and the pebble skimmed across the surface of the water bouncing eight times before it sank to the bottom.

The man with the microphone shouted, "We have a winner."

'The Pebbles Picture' by Donna Roscoe

Help! Help! Hey, you I'm down here can you not see me I'm a little pebble amongst the bigger stones and pebbles. It is hard to see me, but I need to try and get on top and away before that cold horrible dirty salty water comes along and pushes us all around.

Swishing and swirling we will go. I get quite dizzy when this starts, not knowing where I will land or who will land on top of me with a bump. This can go on for hours and hours and I do end up feeling quite sick. It's great when that cold wet salty stuff goes away, I can rest if these stones and pebbles aren't piled on top.

Sometimes noisy happy people come along and pick me up and throw me for miles skimming that cold wet salty stuff. Then plop! In I go down, down, deep into the dark cold salty water into wet sand. I stay here until some big foot stands on me and yelps! They've hurt their foot on my head but that's their fault not mine. This big hand reaches down and picks me up and throws me way up high shouting words I do not want here again. Plop! Here I go again down, down deep in to the salty, murky dirty water.

This time I know it's going to take a while to get back to shore to bathe in the sun again with all other pebbles and stones.

'Pebbles' by Cilla Shiels

Many moons ago, I sold many jars of sweets to local schoolchildren. Among the usual pear drops, aniseed balls and dolly mixtures, we sold the more bizarre-sounding Space Dust, Pebbles and Jawbreakers. The Space Dust was in sachets which the children opened up and swallowed the contents of i.e., 'dust'. This powder reacted on their saliva, making an involuntary popping sound in their mouths. The Pebbles looked exactly like the pebbles we picked off the beach and were rock hard to bite into. I dare say many a child might have lost a tooth or two through eating those strange-looking sweets, but we never had any complaints!

My inquisitive mind got the better of me when the Jawbreakers (a 2.5cm sphere gumball) were being sold in their hundreds. I wanted to know why they were so popular. In answer to my eagerness to find out, I bit into the hard outer shell of the sweet, tasting the delicious blackcurrant flavour. I started chewing the inner bubble gum and got my comeuppance. Out came a large filling from my back tooth. My curiosity cost me a visit to the dentist.

I gave the Jawbreakers a wide berth from thereon.

'Treat A Pebble with Respect' by Joan Isherwood

Do not meddle with a pebble
You don't know where it has been.
If you meddle with a pebble
Magic may occur unseen.

Collect your pebbles, do not peddle,
Treat with care – just like a medal.
All shapes and sizes to admire,
Store them to your heart's desire.

Put some polish on a pebble,
Bring out its colours – make it shine.
Reveal its past like a fine wine,
Paint it, etch it, be a rebel.

On the beach you'll find some pebbles,
Rolling up with each fresh tide.
Fill your bucket – double, treble,
Tip them out and watch them slide.

Young children should not play with pebbles.
Treat a pebble with respect.
Eat it at your utmost peril.
Obey the rule, be safe – protect.

'Distant Shores by Beryl Loy

John tidied his desk for the last time and walked out and down to the river front. It was six o' clock and John had worked in his father's office for five long years, doing an apprenticeship, learning the ins and out of the import/export trade of Jeremiah and Sons. Before that, he had worked for five years in the Sea Cadets, learning the ropes, tides, and sails and how to keep ships afloat and seaworthy.

All his life he had lived in the family home in Waterloo, watching ships sail past, yachts turning and tacking. He spent many hours on the beach as a lad, throwing pebbles into the lapping water, listening to the sounds of the sea. The crashing waves in the storms, the gentle lapping of the tides ebbing and flowing on good days, the cry of the sea birds. He loved the salty smell of the ozone and the tang of the sea breeze.

Now he was working at the dockside in the city and the sights were of men from every tribe and nation, some in strange attire, pouring off the ocean-going vessels, looking for cheap lodgings and whatever else they could buy on their meagre wages. The sounds now, were of men's' voices. Their languages were so different, so musical, and rhythmical. Stevedores' shouting orders to the dockers loading and unloading cargos and Captains' shouting "anchors away!"

John walked down to the water's edge, as he had done many times before, and watched the tide bringing in flotsam and jetsam. He imagined it had floated all the way from Jamaica or Morocco, although he knew it could be from Birkenhead, the other side of the busy River Mersey. He watched the forest of masts swaying to the rhythm of the water, some with sails open and being pushed along by the winds. John walked home along the riverside to eat with the family. He didn't know when he would eat a meal with them again. River life had always filled his young head with curiosity about what the world was like. What where its sights and sounds, its attractions, its aromas?

Now John had a place on his father's ship, the 'Northern Mermaid', and the family's blessings. He lay in his bed that night, unable to sleep. His mind was going through the procedures and the paperwork in his bag, knowing that they were signed, sealed and correct.

All was ship-shape and Bristol fashion. Tomorrow, John's hard work would come to fruition, and he would be on his way at last. He did eventually, drift off to sleep, dreaming of distant shores and unknown lands.

'Love 1' by Karen Wadsworth

"I love you. No, no don't say it, because I know it's not true. Don't worry about me, it's not that all-encompassing, desperate love anymore. I love you less than I did last week and probably more than I will next week.

I'm know I haven't got your exclusive attention, so every time you cancel our dates or turn up late, I love you a little less. Make the most of me while I still care something about you. I reckon you have between one to three months before I get fed up with you sleeping around.

I think it's already too late to come back from this. I'm not sure I'll ever be able to trust you again.

So do we have dinner, or do you want to leave now?"

'Love 2' by Karen Wadsworth

Oh no she's said she loves me again, maybe I should say it back to her, make her feel good. What, she loves me less than before? She can't mean it; I give her attention.

Ah, she knows, but what's a guy supposed to do when it's offered on a plate to him. I'm only human, they mean nothing, just sex.

She's going to dump me. No, please. She's the best thing that's happened to me. I don't want to lose her. Please don't say it's too late, I'll give up the girls. I think I really do love her. Please let me change her mind.

"I'd like to stay for dinner, if that's okay with you."

'Holiday' by John Timmis

"Tickets please?"
Jack hurried to the Seatown gate, ticket in hand.
"Morning sir," the inspector said with a smile as he took the proffered ticket. He examined it closely. His smile vanished. "I'm sorry sir - this ticket is invalid. I cannot let you through."
"It can't be - I've only just bought it - over there." Jack pointed the ticket windows.
"Then you will need to take it up with them," he said curtly, handing it back, "I can't allow you to board."
"But….?" Jack began to protest, putting his holiday case down. The inspector waved him away pointing to the ticket office and motioning to the queue of people with tickets in hand waiting.
"You must be mistaken," Jack argued, offering the ticket again.
"No, sir - I am not mistaken. Now would you please stand aside?"
Reluctantly, Jack grabbed his case and made a beeline for the ticket office.

"The ticket inspector said this ticket was invalid," Jack said sharply handing it to the man behind the window.

"Quite right," the man replied through pursed lips, "this ticket was issued last week and is no longer valid."

"But I bought it here at the ticket office no more than an hour ago."

The man looked at his watch then straightened.

"It was certainly bought at 8.30 am - but not 8.30 am today. It is clearly dated Friday **last** week." The teller placed it carefully out of reach, his other hand reached under the counter.

"I was served by a lady - I can clearly remember her." Jack tried to keep calm.

"The only lady who works here has finished her shift."

Jack was suddenly aware of two uniformed men standing at each side of him.

"Would you please accompany us to the office so that we may look into this matter sir?"

"Why…?' Jack gasped in surprise.

"Please?" One of them repeated, turning. A further surprise awaited Jack at the office. Two policemen were already there.

"Please sit." One of them indicated a chair at the far end of the table. "I am Detective Chief Inspector Brown," he announced. "Before we continue, I should warn you that anything you say may be taken down and used in evidence against you. Empty your pockets onto the table. Put your case over there."

"But I've done nothing wrong," Jack asserted, shaking his head.

"What is your full name, address, and postcode?" The police inspector then turned his laptop so that Jack could see the screen. It showed a video of the exchange at the platform gate. "Is this you?"

"Yes, of course it is." Jack failed to hide the irritation in his voice. The inspected produced a ticket now in an evidence bag.

"Who gave you this ticket?"

"The lady at the ticket office counter of course."

"Did you pay by card or cash?"

"Cash." The detective nodded, frowning.

"What did this lady look like?"

"Errr - I didn't take that much notice."

"But you said to the inspector at the station that you 'clearly remembered being served by a lady'

"Who else was there?"

"I don't remember seeing anyone else."

"The lady teller from the early shift does not remember selling any tickets for Seatown this morning," the inspector said with slow deliberation." He stood up. "Jack Wilson, I am charging you with attempted fraud. You will be held in custody pending further investigations. Take him away. C cell."

'Heaven' by Donna Roscoe

I believe heaven is a nice place to go

Full of sunshine and pearly golden gates

Marshmallow, fluffy white clouds with nice clear blue sky

If this was true, there would be one big queue around the world

Fighting to be next in line; will it be you?

Heaven spelt backwards is a lovely girl's name Nevaeh

I know a little teenager called Nevaeh

Looking at her, she is a stunner

Young, quiet girl, with dark hair and pale complexion

A model she would make,

Let's see what the future holds…

We hope you enjoyed reading our work as much as

the pleasure we had in writing it.

'All Seasons' Writing Group

You may wish to meet with us for a 'taster session'. You will be made most welcome for a chat and refreshments.

You will meet other like-minded folk who just want to put pen to paper.

This will give you an opportunity to decide if it's what you were looking for.

Cilla Shiels

If you would like to join our group, ,please telephone the Volunteer Co-ordinator for details:

Tel: (01925) 240064

Printed in Great Britain
by Amazon